Plots from

Literary Estates

Plots from Literary Estates

The Best and Worst of Al Cline

by

Alan Cline

LitEstates Publishing   Columbus

LitEstates

Publishing

Plots from Literary Estates: The Best and Worst of Al Cline

ISBN 978-1-7367336-4-6

All language content is original to the author and without help from any AI tool. However, illustrations inside and on the cover are produced with the help of OpenAI's GPT-3. They require this accreditation:

> The author generated all illustrations in part with GPT-3, OpenAI's large-scale language-generation model. Upon generating draft images, the author reviewed, edited, and revised them to his own liking and takes ultimate responsibility for the content of this publication.

Dedicated with appreciation to Julie, Katie, and Carolyn for their support and suggestions; and to my wife Carol for her support and toleration for the time I spent in my man-cave working.

Table of Contents

Fantasy Story

I have been a game designer for decades, particularly for fantasy role playing games. I have over 600 scripts of that sort on my back shelves, many of which I've written myself. It is natural that I would write a few fantasy stories.

I like fantasy stories, but they sometimes get too free-wheeling and superficial; perhaps because fantasy is often written for children and treated like fairy tales. Too often the ending is *deus ex machina*: super-person saves the day. It seems lazy that the author could not find a workable solution to the problem facing the characters of the story; or perhaps the author follows the heroic myth trope where the hero *must* save the day.

Boy Wizard tells the story of a street urchin taken in by a kind mage and teaches him (and us) about magic. What would I feel if I went to a school that taught magic? I wanted my readers to feel that ambience, to feel the forces on a child in that environment. I also used some of the vast potential from novels by T.H. White and Sir Thomas Malory about King Arthur. This is perhaps my favorite story in the collection, which is why I put it first.

1

Plots from Literary Estates

Boy Wizard

First Meeting

The old man sat alongside the road and looked forward to his daily meal, a bowl of rice and a chunk of cheese. A shabby brown robe beneath a woolen hat enclosed him. Various small feathers stuck out from his hat and shook whenever a slight breeze passed by. Scraps of colored cloth and other oddments protruded from his person as well; even a small spider hung out near his right ear. His leathery face and beard built a façade around alert black eyes that were constantly in motion.

A fifteen-year old boy appeared in front of him from around a bend in the road. "Hey mister," he said. "How'd you like to see some magic?" He was a ragamuffin— raggedy clothes, hair askew, dirt covering parts of his face and arms. His eyes sparkled and he emanated joy and adventure.

The old man looked up from his bowl, impatient at

3

being interrupted before he could eat. He examined the boy. "You know magic, do you?" he said in a creaky voice.

The boy was taken aback a second. That was not the response to which he was accustomed. Most people shook their head or stepped away; others threatened him with a swat if he didn't leave them alone. He recovered quickly.

"Sure, I know magic, as I will demonstrate right now."

"And what kind of magic do you know?" the old man continued his calm inquisition.

The boy had not heard that question before. *What kind of magic? What kinds were there?* "Well, I'll show you." He produced a wooden coin apparently from thin air. "I can make something disappear," he beguiled.

"Hmph!" The old man scoffed.

The boy tossed the coin into the air. The man reflexively glanced up at the ascending coin. As he did so, the boy slipped the bowl from the old man's hands and ran down the lane, laughing.

A dark scowl flashed over the old man's face. He shot out a finger, pointing at the fleeing figure. *"Pariplu!"* A small wavering of air gathered around the boy and he rose a dozen inches from the ground, causing him to lose traction. His momentum continued to carry him forward another few feet, but although his legs kept running, his escape down the trail slowed to a stop.

The old man grunted as he rose from his sitting position and walked toward the boy, who saw him coming and tried to run faster. His legs flailed but he went nowhere. The old man stood beside him and looked at

4

him.

"How do you like *my* magic?" the wizard asked the confused boy.

Embarrassed, the boy stopped struggling for a moment, then tried to run again, to no avail. He reached for the old man who stepped back out of reach.

"Let me down, mister," the boy gasped. "I didn't mean no harm."

"No harm, eh? That is my only meal for today. Would you have me starve on the road?"

The boys eyes flickered, trying to conjure an answer to that. "I'm hungry too," he finally spat out.

"Hmm." The man stroked his beard thoughtfully and studied the boy. "Where are you from? Where are your parents?"

"I don't know. I don't have any."

The old man doubted that, but obviously, this urchin had been living in poverty for some time.

"What's your name?" the man pressed on.

"I don't know."

"What do your friends call you?"

"I don't have any friends," the boy replied. He stared angrily at the old man. His jaw lowered and set.

"Hmm," the wizard said again. He sighed and leaned back on his heels. "So that's how you're going to play it, eh?"

The old man took a deep breath, pursed his lips, and came to a conclusion. "I'll tell you what. I'm going to give you an opportunity. If you are as smart as I think you are, you'll take it." He paused to let that sink in.

The boy tilted his head slightly, wary of what might come next.

"I'm going to let you down and you can run away down that trail...or you can come with me. You will have daily food and shelter. It's up to you." While the boy was thinking about that, the old man reached through the wavering air and plucked his bowl from the boy.

Not seeming to notice the missing bowl, the boy looked at himself as he hovered a foot above the dirt path. He scanned the wavering air around him. He hopped up and down a little. He was stuck and he knew it. "What's in it for you?" the boy demanded.

"You will be my helper. You will work and do whatever I tell you to do. You'll have a place to stay and a community. And if you don't work out..." he paused for effect and emphasized the last word, "I can always turn you into a *toad*."

The boy's eyes first widened in surprise and then narrowed in disbelief. The old man's eyes sparkled and a smile played on his lips. The boy knew the old man was jesting. The wizard snapped his fingers, turned and started to walk back to his original location beside the trail with his bowl.

The sphere of air disappeared and the boy gently descended to the ground. As soon as his feet touched the ground, he sprinted down the trail and out of sight of the old wizard.

The wizard heard him go and shook his head sadly. He

plodded back to his original place at the side of the road and sat his old body smoothly on the ground again. He started to put rice in his mouth.

A shadow fell over the old man as the boy returned and stood beside him. The boy watched the rice and cheese hungrily.

The wizard stared at the boy for a moment, then nodded. An understanding had been reached. "Sit!" he commanded.

The boy dropped down beside him.

The old man pulled an empty battered drinking cup from his robes and put half the rice into it. He broke off half the cheese and put that into the cup and then passed the cup to the boy, who scarfed it down in seconds.

The wizard finished his half-meal slowly, not saying a word. When he was done, he poured a little water into the drinking cup for the boy, then himself. He rose, brushed off any dirt from his robes, and picked up a gnarled walking stick that lay beside him. The old man ambled down the trail. "Come along."

The two new acquaintances traveled together on the trail without words. If anyone had been near to see them, they would have thought that these two vagrants had traveled together for a long time.

First Secret

The old man and the boy wandered up the trail for several hours. The forested trail turned to the rocky terrain of foothills, which turned to a passage into the mountains. It snaked through high canyons and narrow ledges, constantly rising. They saw few passersby in this desolate area. The sun was descending for the night, projecting shadows on the cliffside walls. The evening threatened to quickly turn cold and dark.

The wizard stopped near a house-size protrusion of granite that forced the trail to curve around it. "Can you keep a secret?" he said without preamble.

The boy had been lost in his own thoughts about magic and how this old man made him float above the ground. *Could I learn to do that?* he thought. The wizard's question pulled him from his reverie. "What?"

"This is your first duty. Can you keep a secret?" The dark eyes, deep within hollow sockets above leathery wrinkles, stared down at the boy, searching him.

"As good as anyone else, I guess." The boy's brows furrowed in puzzlement.

"That says little," the old man huffed. "Some people rattle on about whatever pops into their head and they usually reveal how little they know. Others are so tight-lipped you don't know that they have a secret." He looked over at the boy. "Can you be one of those?"

What the old man meant to reveal to him still eluded the boy but the severity of his statement was clear. The boy nodded.

"What I am about to show you is important. Keep this to yourself. I'm trusting you." He paused until the boy nodded.

"This will be our first secret," the old man said. "If not, we part ways here and now."

The boy nodded again, this time anxious to learn the secret.

The wizard approached the wall and raised one hand. "*Kavas*" he spoke to it.

A grating sound of rock-on-rock disrupted the quiet evening air. A ten-foot section of granite wall facing the wizard slid aside, revealing a three-foot wide doorway and a chamber within. The boy couldn't help himself but step around the wizard and peer inside.

The old man pulled him back a little and stuck a finger over his lips. The wizard concentrated his gaze on the boy and gave a questioning dip of his head, as if to say "Can you keep a secret?" The boy nodded and let the man pass first into the chamber.

The room was a cavity in the rock, cool from a pool of water off to one side. A spring fountained from a side wall into the pool. A set of rock steps ascended upward out of sight.

The wizard turned around, facing outward. "*Gadha.*" The stone door slid shut with the same grating sound it had made when it opened. The boy wondered what would happen if he wanted to leave. He didn't know how to open this magical door.

His mild alarm turned to curiosity as he walked to the bottom of the steps and peered upward. Despite being inside a rock room, there was light at the top of the stairs —fifty, one hundred, two hundred steps above.

The old man began the steep climb up the stairs. The boy followed, placing his feet carefully on the tread of the worn rock.

The steps were old, worn with the passage of many years of uncounted feet that had passed this way. Each stone step was slightly curved downward in the middle from wear. The footfalls of the two travelers echoed slightly in the ascending tunnel as they plodded toward the light above. The boy wondered how this staircase came to be. He couldn't see where anyone had chiseled or cut the rock, but someone had made this tunnel of stairs. *More magic?* the boy asked himself.

Eventually, the roof wall gave way to open air and evening light, the stairs ended on a flat platform. The old man leaned on this walking stick at the top of the stairs, breathing only slightly harder than he had on the trail outside.

The boy came up behind him breathing heavily. After he caught his breath, he peered back down the stairs to check how far they had come. The stairs ended in darkness at the bottom of the tunnel. *Those steps were steep!*

The boy, standing at the landing at the top of the stairs, turned and gazed out across a plaza between a circle of marble buildings. Stone walkways crisscrossed the plaza and led to numerous doors in the buildings. The walkways threaded their way between trees arrayed in dirt areas and between magnificent statues of silvery metal or white marble. The setting sun stretched long shadows across the plaza from the statues and trees, giving the entire area a black-and-white enamel of austere beauty.

"Wow!" The boy couldn't believe that such a place existed. "This is beautiful!"

"Not as much as you may think," the old man said matter-of-factly. "Most of it is *glamour* to make the residents feel important. Perhaps at one time it was truly a magnificent campus. Today..." he tsked. "Puff and poof! *Glamour.*"

A few people moved about in the plaza, mostly strolling along the walkways and entering various doors. Many carried scrolls or books by their side. Most of them wore long robes of brown or grey. "What place is this?" the boy asked.

The old man at last smiled, then spoke as if reciting an age-old greeting. As he did so, he waved his arm to indicate the expanse of the plaza. "Welcome to the Arcanium, Academy of Magic!" He returned to his normal voice. "Few people outside the community know about this place, except perhaps as rumor or legend." He proceeded along the left side of the plaza, toward another staircase along the side of a central building.

"Arcane...Acad—? What's that?"

"This is where the students of the arcane arts, or *magic,* come to learn and to practice their skills. This is where you will serve me."

"Is this where I will learn magic?" the boy asked in amazement.

"Ha! Definitely not! You need to be enrolled as a student for that."

11

"Then why am I here?"

"Weren't you listening? You are here to serve me. You're my gofer. You agreed to it on the forest trail. Right?" The old man turned to look at the boy, his head tilted.

"Right," the boy replied. "What's a gopher?"

"Well, you go for this, and go for that. You know, a gofer."

The boy quit smiling, his head drooped. He nodded. *Was he a prisoner here? A slave? What if he wanted to run away and didn't like what this old man wanted him to do?* Then he thought of the chamber at the bottom of the stairs. He didn't know how to open the rock wall door to escape anyway. *He was trapped here.*

As they moved along the rock pathway, another person in a brown robe approached. "Merl," the robed figure said in greeting.

"Lester," the old man acknowledged.

"How was your quest," Lester asked.

"It was successful. And look, a bonus. I got a boy," the old man said.

"Very good," Lester nodded without looking down at the boy. Then Lester and the old man continued on past each other without further conversation.

"You're name is Merl?" the boy asked.

"No, Merl is my title. I am the leader of this community."

"Well, what's your name?" the boy asked.

"You can call me Merl. I prefer Sir. You want to know

12

my name and yet have not told me yours. Very well, I will call you 'Boy'. Yes, that will do quite nicely."

The boy didn't know if he liked that or not, but in truth, he had not told the old man his name when they first met. But then, he didn't know what the old man had in mind. Now he did, but he couldn't let this slight pass.

"Okay. I will call you 'Old Man'." He glanced over to see how the wizard would react to that. When no response came, he continued, imitating the old man. "Yes, 'Old Man', that will do quite nicely."

"Come, Boy!" The old man walked along the plaza's edge and started up the stairs of the central building.

"Right behind you, Old Man."

First Night

At the top of the stairs, a wide stone porch afforded a view over the central plaza and the valley beyond. A city sparkled in the dusky sunlight far away on the valley floor below. The boy took in the expanse in awe. He was at the top of the world! He also delighted in knowing that he was not trapped here. He could always descent the long stairway toward the city below.

His eyes explored the various buildings around the plaza. Many on the east side reflected the orange light of sunset back into the plaza. Western buildings threw stark grey shadows into the center to mix and merge with the shadows from the trees and statues. Most buildings had a flat roof, but small round turrets with pointed roofs

13

adorned others, extending upward so that they displayed
orange at top, red in the middle, and grayer near the
bottom as the sunlight spread across the turrets.

The old man reached the porch at the top of the stairs.
Without hesitation, he entered through a doorway that led
off from the porch. The doorway could be closed with a
heavy exterior door but now it stood open. From inside
darkness, the old man called back, "Come!" His voice
reverberated in the inner chamber and sounded more
powerful, more ominous.

The boy shook himself and followed. He passed into a
darkened room. It took a moment for his eyes to adjust to
the dimness, but then he saw that he was in a comfortably
furnished apartment. Boy thought about that. *Even when the
Merl is gone, the door to his apartment stood open and unsecured.
What kind of place is this?*

The old man lit a lamp and the light made the shadows
jump away. Wood panels covered rock walls and benches
to one side contained a confusion of devices, half-finished
projects lying about for easy access. The room emanated a
welcoming feeling in sharp contrast to the beautiful but
cold façade of the exterior. Whereas outside the building
was all cold marble and pomp, this inner apartment felt
warm and cozy.

Boy scanned the room. Apparently he was in the
kitchen. A lifeless fireplace with a black cauldron hanging
over it possessed one wall. Metal pans and pots rested on a
stone shelf above it. The room contained three small
tables, one filled with a collection of wooden and metal

devices of which Boy had no idea what they could be. Small glass containers of crushed herbs and colored powders, seasonings he supposed, were arrayed on a shelf above the table. A second table contained smaller items, an ink bottle and quill, and a red-covered book. The third and largest table was empty. Two chairs sat beside it.

A horizontal ring of wood that could have served as a chandelier hung from the ceiling, except that instead of a lantern or a set of candles, strands of garlic and onions hung from small hooks along its circumference. Also hanging from the ring were sprigs of various herbs and small half-filled bags made of a coarse whitish material.

The old man walked into the adjoining room. From where he sat, Boy could see a large bed with thick blankets in the center. Merl took off his robe and hung it on a rack on the wall. Beneath the robe, he was dressed in a well-fitted tunic and leather breeches. A small dagger hung from a leather belt around his waist. The robe hid a more muscular and trim body than one would expect beneath the face and manner of the old man.

Boy realized that the robe was merely an outer garment. *Of course people wear clothes beneath their robe,* he thought, but he had never seen anyone without their robe. In fact, he had seen few people in robes at all. Most people he saw wore cloaks for colder weather. He was familiar with the soldiers who kicked him aside whenever he took refuge along the untended alcoves of the city streets at night or in heavy rains. The red-and-orange uniformed soldiers wore cloaks prepared from animal skins and

15

leather armor beneath that. *Why had I thought the old man wore little underneath?* the boy wondered. He made a mental note to not be fooled by his own assumptions in the future.

A stocky young man appeared in a second doorway on the other side of the kitchen. "I saw your light," the man said. "Welcome back."

"Thank you, Edmund," Merl said. "Please fix me something to eat. I've traveled far today. And yes, fix something for him too. I got this boy on the journey."

Edmund raised one eyebrow.

"I think he can take over some of your chores here. Give you more time for your studies."

"Thank you," Edmund replied. A broad smile lit up his face. "The term is getting harder and does require more time. I appreciate the time to spend with my studies. My Amalgams teacher showed me a great cantrip. It was so simple, I never would have--"

"Okay, okay, Edmund," Merl interrupted. "You can tell me about it tomorrow. Tonight, we need food and rest." He dropped into a chair at the empty table and gestured for Boy to sit.

"Of course, Merl." Edmund ran from the doorway and returned in a few minutes with an armful of foodstuffs. "With you gone all month, we have less than usual in the pantry."

Although he sounded as if he delivered bad news, his face still carried a wide grin. He bustled about the kitchen and threw down on the table two wooden bowls, cheese,

16

dried meat, dried apples, a few turnips and beets, and a wooden bottle of something. Edmund placed these all precisely on the table in front of Merl and the boy. He paused when he was about to place a knife within reach of Boy.

"For him too, sir?" Edmund asked.

Old Man chuckled and looked at the almost-salivating boy. "You're not going to kill me in my sleep, are you?"

Boy was dumbfounded by the remark. The idea had never entered his mind. He was staring at the small feast being laid out in front of him. Before he could answer, Merl nodded slightly and Edmund placed the knife in the center of the table.

Merl took a swig from the wooden bottle and stopped. He looked up at Edmund. "We'll need some water too. This ale is not appropriate for him."

Edmund pulled a deep bowl from a shelf along one wall and walked to the far end of the room, which was still in dimness. For the first time, Boy noticed a large water-filled trough in an alcove, a trough large enough for him to take a bath in. Edmund submerged the bowl in a single smooth motion and returned with it to the table, still dripping.

"Thank you, Edmund." Merl had already popped a few pieces of cheese into his mouth and started to cut into the dried meat. "Tomorrow we will talk about what chores you can pass on to Boy. See you in the morning."

Edmund nodded and as quickly as he had appeared in the doorway earlier, he was gone.

Merl and Boy ate in silence. Merl seemed to relish the peace and quiet at his return to home and Boy was too hungry to worry about conversation. He had not seen this much food within his reach for a month.

After Boy had eaten until he thought his stomach would burst, he sat back in his chair tired, relaxed and happy. A burp escaped from his lips that made him smile.

Merl startled, as if he had forgotten about his dinner partner while he was deep in thought. He took a deep breath. "Well, I guess we should find you a place to sleep."

He picked the lamp from the table and walked toward an alcove. Boy thought he could be comfortable enough sleeping on a stone bench within the kitchen alcove, a kitchen that would be warm from a lit fireplace during the colder days.

Surprisingly, the alcove was actually a small doorway at the top of a narrow set of stone stairs. Merl explained as they descended, "This building, in fact, the entire Academy, was originally a monastery for a long forgotten religion. My predecessors repurposed it decades ago. Since it is the largest building, the Merl gets use of it but I rarely find need to come down here."

The steps ended in a narrow stone pathway between a set of doors that ran alongside the passage. Each door had a small square opening at face height, perhaps for a window pane to be included or a small set of bars. To the boy, it seemed like a prison.

Merl stopped to light a torch in a cresset on the wall. "You can have the room closest to the bottom of the stairs

18

here." He opened a thick wooden door. Boy peered inside
to see a cot with a straw mattress and a thin woolen
blanket, a small wooden table with a candleholder in it, and
a chamber pot nearby. "I've had a guest here before, a time
or two."

The boy noticed that the door had a latch and could
be locked from either side. From the height of the square
hole in the door, he knew he would not be able to reach
through to unlock the door, even if he had a key for it. A
prison, he decided. The old man waited.

Boy stepped one foot inside but did not put both feet
in. He braced himself if Merl decided to give him a sudden
push into the room. "Okay, thanks," he feigned.

"We start at dawn." Merl turned and left him to
himself and ascended the stairs.

Boy was not sure what to do. He knew he couldn't lie
down on the cot to sleep lest someone come by in the
night and lock him in. The first thing was to disable the
lock. He took the torch from the cresset and lit the candle
from the small table. He melted some wax and jammed a
wadded up glob of it into the latch. That should stop the
door from locking for a few minutes at least, until they
figured it out.

Then he realized that he didn't want to sleep in the
bottom of a stone castle anyway. He was used to sleeping
outside, which is perhaps not the most accommodating,
but it was under the stars and in the fresh air.

He crept up the stairs silently and past Merl's
bedroom, where he heard the soft sound of snoring. He

wandered outside into the cool night air. Near the center of the plaza below, he saw several apple trees with comfortable horizontal branches. He had slept in trees before: good at staying above forest predators at night, good for the fresh air, and good for seeing enemies coming from a distance. He crawled onto one of the branches well above the ground and was soon asleep.

First Day

Ow! Something stabbed at Boy's legs, a prickly pain that ran up and down his body.

"Get outta me tree," a gravelly voice shouted at him from below.

Boy snapped awake. It was early morning. He remembered he had slept in a tree so he was careful not to fall out. He looked down at a grizzled old man in heavy clothing, his hand resting on a small cart of seedlings, dirt, and gardening supplies.

"Get outta me tree!" the grizzled man shouted again. He pointed his hand at Boy and flared the fingers of his right hand. Small bluish lightning bolts shot from his hand and struck Boy.

The pain flashed up and down the boy's body and he gasped for breath. He scrambled to get down from the tree but was having trouble moving his legs.

"Ya dink trees grow by demselves!" the old man shouted.

This puzzled the boy. "Well, eh, …yes," the boy

replied.

"Smart ass!" Another wave of fiery bolts hit him as he tried to get down and he fell from the tree onto his side.

"Oof!" The boy grabbed a quick breath and limped away from the tree. "Sorry, I didn't know this was your tree."

"Gorbal!" Merl shouted from the porch above. "Let him be. He's new here. He's with me."

Startled, the grizzled man looked up at the academy chief. "Don't care if he's new here or who he's wit'," but he wasn't adamant about his defiance. "He got no business in me trees. Probably stealing me apples, I bet."

"As delicious as your apples are, Gorbal, he wasn't stealing your apples." Merl called to the boy, "You weren't stealing his apples, were you?"

Boy shook his head vigorously as he looked at Gorbal.

Merl called out again to Boy. "Come up here. We've been looking for you."

The boy was happy to leave this curmudgeon behind, so he limped to the bottom of Merl's stairs and ascended. He could hear Gorbal grumbling under his breath about his trees and his apples and the abuse of power some Merls exercised. His grumbling became fainter as Boy moved away. The pain and numbness in his legs quickly subsided as Boy climbed the steps.

"We've been looking all about, wondering where you went. Why did you sleep out here?" Merl asked.

Boy was not sure how to answer. He didn't want to say he didn't trust Merl, or that he thought he would be locked away in the dungeon of the cell they gave him as his room. He didn't like being shelved in with the other underground cells, like some sort of crypt for the living. "Well, I'm used to sleeping outside, under the stars," he answered.

Merl tilted his head and stared at him with one eye for what seemed to Boy an eternity, as if searching inside the boy for the truth. Merl nodded. "Okay, we can set you up with something temporarily. Will this porch work for you? It's outside but under cover of weather—until it gets too cold."

Boy scanned the porch at the top of the stairs overlooking the plaza below: a flat expanse on either side of the door with a stout roof overhead but open on the sides. He could see the mountains in the distance and the golden city in the valley below. He nodded.

Merl turned and walked inside. "Edmund, let's move Boy's room outside." He turned to Boy who had followed him into the apartment. "Edmund will help."

Edmund was in the middle of making breakfast. He sighed, put down a container of liquid and a pan suspended by iron bars over the fire, and descended the stairs. Boy followed as quickly as he could down the stone stairs.

Edmund tossed off the hay mattress and lifted the bed's wooden frame onto his shoulders and steadied it with one hand. He took it upstairs, leaving Boy to wonder what to do next. Boy threw the thin woolen blanket aside and lifted the mattress with a grunt and pulled it outside the cell. It kept touching the floor on one end and stopping his progress. It bumped against the doorjamb, forcing him back a step.

The mattress wasn't especially heavy but it was awkward. He could find no good handhold. He decided to leave it and picked up the small table and candlestick instead. He threw the blanket over his shoulder. He was at the bottom of the stairs when Edmund returned.

"Grab that end." Edmund motioned to the far side of the mattress. Boy set the table and candlestick on the stone floor and ran to the other side of the mattress. Edmund grabbed the mattress and ascended the stairs, pulling Boy along. Boy struggled to keep up as the mattress rose up the stairwell in front of him. Edmund could have carried the mattress by himself but Boy was helping.

Once outside on the porch, Edmund dropped the mattress without ceremony on the wooden frame that now sat on the porch a few yards from the main door to Merl's apartment. He returned to the kitchen and continued with breakfast.

Boy threw off the blanket from his shoulder and onto the mattress. He ran back downstairs for the small table and candlestick. He placed those to the side of his bed. He looked around. *Whew! Done! What else did he need? Water in the morning but that was inside the kitchen. Chamber pot?* He returned to his "bedroom" at the bottom of the stairs, retrieved the chamber pot, and placed it between the bed frame and the wall of the porch. Boy had never used a chamber pot before, so he didn't think he needed it.

23

Beside, those trees down there would serve him fine...
until he remembered Gorbal. Boy decided to choose a
different target than Gorbal's trees.

He adjusted the mattress and spread the blanket over
it. He sat on the edge and looked out across the Arcanium
campus. He thought this was a good place to sleep, but
then he realized that everyone could see him. He was
sleeping out in view of a crowd. Oh well, didn't matter.
Anyone could see him when he slept on the streets too. At
least he wasn't sleeping in a stone cell.

Merl called out from inside. "Boy! Food if you want it.
You have a busy day ahead of you."

Boy smiled to himself and went into the apartment.
The food smelled great, but he couldn't identify it.
Whatever it was, he ate a great amount of it while Merl
explained the day for him.

After breakfast, Edmund showed Boy the chores that
he would be taking from Edmund. It wasn't much. Boy
would not have to cook meals or do any heavy lifting. Merl
took care of himself mostly. Now and then, Edmund
trimmed Merl's beard, but Edmund opined that Boy might
not be asked to do that, seeing that Boy was so young.

"Perhaps Merl will do that himself and not risk a
mistake that could injure his, er...dignity. He is a Merl after
all and has to show the proper image around the
academy," Edmund explained.

At one point, Edmund showed Boy the clothes in
Merl's closet. For a boy on the streets who slept in a single
set of clothes week after week, Boy wondered why anyone

needed so many robes. Merl must have three or four robes, all of slightly different colors. Sandals and sturdier walking shoes lined the bottom of the closet.

Merl had a thick winter coat padded with some kind of animal skin. Boy remembered the times he shivered in the cold, trying to get close to fires the hoodlums lit. He stared at the winter coat and imagined what it would feel like to snuggle into its soft luxuriousness.

"Do you think you can do what Edmund showed you?" Merl asked.

Boy shrugged. "Doesn't seem hard." He said this without thinking, without any ill intent, but Edmund gave him a dark glare.

"I was going to ask Edmund to give you a tour of the campus, but I need to run an errand this morning. I'll give you the tour myself."

Edmund let out an exaggerated sigh of relief, perhaps in retaliation for Boy's comment.

Merl suppressed a smile but his eyes twinkled, which gave him away. "You'll be running errands and delivering messages for me mostly. You need to get acquainted with the locations of the shops and the people you will deal with. Be ready to leave in ten minutes."

Boy looked around. He walked outside and looked at his bed. He was ready to leave. He had nothing else to do. He spied Gorbal's orchard in the plaza below and thought of the apples on the tree. They were ripe and they shined in the sunlight, but he thought better of taking any and left them alone.

Eventually, Merl bustled from the apartment and strode down the stairs. "Come" was his only comment. Across the plaza and to the top of the wide steps that overlooked the valley and the city below, he went. The steps were a hundred feet wide and cut directly into the mountain. At the far bottom—a mile away in Boy's estimation—the steps turned into a wide road that led directly into the grid of buildings, and thoroughfares that ran between them. He could see tiny movements in the distance that were carts and people and horses.

Boy could not see what lie on the mountain to the far side of the stairway; but on the near side, the side that he could see, a dirt road meandered back and forth on its way down the mountain. A series of switchbacks allowed wheeled vehicles like horse-drawn wagons to come and go without taking the bump of the steps. The road stopped about one hundred feet below the level of the plaza.

"The capitol city of Thentis," Merl said without preamble, waving his hand at the city. "The king lives there. He's practically the Academy's sponsor. We do him favors from time to time and he helps us out when we need it." He looked down at Boy the street urchin. "You'll probably never meet him," he said flatly.

Merl turned left and walked down a wide series of steps toward the road. At the bottom, the road and steps met at a series of wide terraces that ringed this side of the mountain. Horse corrals aligned the wall. Around the corner, a wooden stable occupied the center of the terrace width. What horses that weren't in the corrals were in stalls

26

in the stable.

Merl strode into the stables and called out. "Hiram! You here?" A muscular, leathery-faced man emerged from a stall. He pulled a rag hanging over a stall partition and rubbed his hands on it. "Good morning, Merl. Welcome back. What can I do you for?"

"Can you have a wagon and horse ready for tomorrow? Just for the day? I'll need to carry some cargo."

Hiram frowned and tilted his head slightly aside. "Sure. For yourself?"

"Yes, but I'll be taking others with me most likely."

"Sure thing. Cart and horse tomorrow."

Merl gave a curt nod. "Oh yes," Merl added. "This is Boy. He's my new, well, boy. Picked him up on my last journey to the low country. He may come to you now and them for errands. I just wanted you to meet him."

Boy thought that was his cue to say something, to introduce himself. He stepped forward, "Glad to meet--"

"Sure," Hiram said, barely looking at him. He threw the rag back on the partition, turned and walked away.

Merl left the stables and walked back to the steps and then back along a higher curved terrace. Boy scrambled to keep up.

A small building made of thick metal fumed black smoke into the air. Tent material formed three walls attached to the metal part of the building. Boy could hear the clang of hammer on metal. He could smell hot iron in the morning sun. Dozens of horseshoes were aligned on two vertical poles, one on each side of the building. He knew a smithy when he heard one—and smelled one.

Before entering, Merl turned and said, "Boy, go back and ask Hiram what time the cart will be ready."

Boy thought that today was a business day. Yesterday was a relaxed day, the return from a hard journey and the welcome ease of being home again. Today, Merl was all business.

"Yes, sir," he replied. He took a couple steps and the feeling arose in him that he was being sent away, not toward a goal but to avoid something. Merl didn't want him about. He had these intuitions before when street thugs were trying to set up an ambush on him or a thief didn't want to share his loot. He checked that Merl wasn't looking and slipped back toward the smithy.

He crept along the terrace with the mountain wall on his left toward the smithy. In the bright sun, he felt exposed and had no good excuse for sneaking about. He looked around to see if he was being watched. He was ten feet above the lower terrace and ten feet below the upper plaza, so unless someone was close on this terrace, he couldn't be seen. Besides, he was Merl's boy. He was invited to be here. Perhaps the best course of action would be to walk to the smithy without sneaking. Then he remembered he was supposed to get a time of day from Hiram. He went back to sneaking along the wall.

Boy continued quietly along the terrace path. He approached the canvas-and-metal structure silently. He could hear Merl and a gruff voice talking. He shifted until he could see through a slit where the tent flaps didn't quite meet. He looked into a smithy, as he expected. Apparently the smith was in the middle of forging something when Merl interrupted him.

He could see Merl and a huge man talking. The smith's muscled arms bulged from a leather vest and above a leather apron. Sweat around a smoldering set of dark eyes in a strong-looking face streamed into his thick reddish beard.

Merl unfolded an old cloth and revealed what looked like a long angular rock in his hand and showed it to the smith. The rock was shiny black and a dull red glow emanated from inside it.

"Where was that found?" the huge man asked in surprise.

"A peasant found it at the base of the mountain, near the Drini River," Merl replied. "He brought it to me, as well he should."

"Did he know what it was?"

"No, I don't think so, or he may not have brought it to me. Or maybe he did, which is *why* he brought it to me."

"That's no good, finding ankigene on the surface like that." The smith's voice was solemn.

"Yes, I know," Merl replied. "I think it does not bode well for the Academy."

Without breaking from the conversation, the smith grabbed up a flat bar of metal and flung it across the tent. It bounced off the dirt, under the tent flap, and up again into Boy's shin. Boy fell down in agony. The smith rushed out, "A spy. We have a spy here."

Merl quickly rewrapped the black stone and followed behind the smith. They saw Boy rocking back and forth holding his shin.

"No, that's my new boy," Merl said. "And a disobedient boy at that."

"He should he killed, now!"

"No, no. I'll take care of it," Merl replied. "We can finish our conversation later."

The smith glared at the boy and muttered again about killing spies. Merl frowned down at Boy and pursed his lips.

"Walk with me," he commanded sternly. Merl walked back along the terrace to the long steps.

Boy got up painfully and limped behind Merl. Merl sat on the terrace, his legs dangling over the side. Boy sat down beside him in similar fashion. He rubbed his shin and looked down at the terrace below and the steps to his right leading down to the golden city.

"He could have broken it, you know," Merl began, not looking at Boy. "If he hadn't bounced that iron off the ground, you would be hobbling on a broken leg and that would be no good. You would have been laid up for some time. You wouldn't be my boy, my gofer, anymore. I need a gofer that can, ah, go."

Boy merely continued to rub his shin.

"What time will Hiram have the cart ready tomorrow?" Merl asked as if it was a routine question.

Boy looked down at his shin. "Ah, I didn't get around to asking him," he murmured.

"I know!" Merl almost thundered. He snapped around to focus directly on Boy. "You had one errand today and instead, you decided to spy on me and my business."

At the word "spy," Boy remembered the smith's threat about killing spies. His eyes went wide and he went still.

"Look, boy," Merl continued. "I am the leader of this Academy. There are many enemies and secrets involved with this job. I need someone I can trust. If I cannot trust you, then you best be on your way." He pointed to the steps. "You can go down into Thentis. There are plenty of people there who follow their own rules, make bad decisions, and live short lives."

Boy considered the stairs down. "I-I-I thought you were just trying to get rid of me," Boy stammered.

"Of course I was trying to get rid of you!" Merl retorted. "You don't need to know all my business, especially about this. If people were to find out, it could start a panic. You must keep this to yourself. Promise?" Merl turned and glared at him.

Boy nodded.

Merl continued more calmly. "If you're going to run errands for me, you are going to hear a lot of information that should stay between us. Can you guarantee that?"

Boy nodded again.

"I deliberately didn't ask Hiram about when the cart would be ready so that I could send you back while I talked with Vulcan. Even so, I could easily have sent a messenger anytime today to ask him." He paused. "Oh wait! I did, and the messenger didn't do it."

31

Boy was abashed. "I'm sorry," was all he could say. All was quiet between the boy and his chief for a minute or two, then, Boy asked shyly, "What is hanky-gene?"

Merl breathed in a deep breath and out again. "That is the secret, Boy. And one secret leads to a desire for more secrets. Suffice to say that ankigene should not be here and that it is an omen of dangerous things to come. Maybe someday I'll tell you, but for now, let's see if you can keep this secret. Best if you forget you heard that name."

- * -

The remainder of the day Merl moved about the Academy, introducing Boy to various merchants, carpenters, gardeners, wagon-makers, rope-winders, coopers, and others. The Academy was a school in appearance but a small town in function. Boy learned where the dormitories were for those who lived on campus. At the bottom of the mountain were houses for others; sometimes for the married students, although that was rare. The King supported and defended the houses because more than students lived there, but Merl was responsible for all properties in the Arcanium at the top of the mountain, including the dormitories.

Near the end of the day, Merl took Boy to a large building at one side of the plaza. Inside, it had corridors in all directions. Merl walked along a curved corridor for a bit, then stopped at an intersection with a closed door on one side and an open door on the other. He pointed to the closed door.

"That is the girls' dormitory. Don't ever go in there. There's no telling what an angry group of sorceresses-in-training will do to you."

Boy's eyes went wide and he diligently nodded.

On the other side of the hallway, the door was open. Boy could see a huge room with shelves and shelves of books, scrolls, and stacks of loose papers. The shelves were in tiers from floor to vaulted ceiling. Most shelves were painted in various colors.

Merl stood at the entrance and beamed with pride. "This is the Library, the biggest repository of written magical works in the world—that we know of, of course." Merl moved to a central circular counter.

A man behind the counter studied something with a Y-shaped device that held two lenses. He didn't notice them approach until Merl tapped on the counter.

"Merl," the man said, looking up. "Good to see you again. Welcome back." The man behind the counter was old and thin, with hair sprouting from various spots on his otherwise bald head.

"Haggard, this is my boy. He will be coming here now and then for me. Lend him whatever he asks for, unless it is in the top tier. If he can't get to it, don't give it to him."

Boy didn't understand this. Why couldn't he get to some of the books?

Haggard studied Boy for a few seconds. "Well boy, can you read?"

Boy frowned. "A little. I didn't have much need of

33

reading in Blackrock."

"That's where I found the little urchin," Merl explained.

Boy wasn't sure how he liked being called "little urchin."

"I'll see if I can get him up to speed in reading, Merl continued. "He says he's a fast learner."

Haggard inspected Boy and his ragamuffin clothes. "Hmm," was all Haggard said.

"While I'm here," Merl continued. "I'd like to get a copy of Cutter's Handbook of Igneous and Metamorphic Monoliths. Also, do you have anything on ankigene?"

At that, Boy was alert. Here was that word again. What did it mean and what was so dangerous about a stone?

"Cutter is over on the blue shelf, but ankigene..." Haggard muttered. "Hmm, yes." He raised his hand and motioned at the top shelf where even the long ladders did not reach. A thick book slid from the stacks, across the spacious room, and down into his hand. "This is a reserved book. You'll have to keep it guarded, but you already know that."

"I'll make sure it stays secure." Merl replied. He looked meaningfully down at Boy, "Right?"

Boy, intrigued, merely nodded.

Merl and the boy walked to their quarters but Boy was full of questions he was afraid to ask. Merl must have that piece of ankigene on him somewhere in one of the many pockets of his robe. He would love to look at it—and at the book about ankigenes.

Over dinner Merl asked Edmund if he could give Boy reading lessons. Edmund shrugged but didn't appear to be pleased about the matter. After dinner, Merl said, "Get some rest, Boy. Tomorrow I have a job for you."

First Task

After breakfast the next morning, Merl was busy packing, checking lists he kept in his robe, and assigning tasks as he prepared for another journey. "While I'm gone, I want Edmund to help you read better. I have to see the King," he said.

"You mean about the—" Boy started.

"I have to see the King, Boy!" Merl interrupted with a glare. "No more conversation." Merl looked over at Edmund then back at Boy. "Boy, fill up the bath. It's running low."

Boy looked at the trough-sized metal container of water to one side of the kitchen. Indeed, it was half-full. "From where?"

"Go down the back steps to the fountain. Get your water there," Merl replied. "There's a bucket near the tub."

Boy looked and sure enough, a large wooden bucket sat in the corner between the wall and the tub. He picked up the bucket. "Down the back steps? The two hundred back steps?" Boy asked, unbelieving. "That'll take me *forever.*"

"Then use two buckets." Merl pointed to the bath tub again.

35

Boy looked over and the bucket he had picked up was still in the corner. Then he realized he was holding the first bucket. A second bucket had appeared out of nowhere in the same place. He went over and picked up the second bucket.

"We can work on your reading lesson when I get back from class," Edmund said. "And when you're done with the tub."

Merl nodded, picked up his supplies, stuffed them into his robe, and left the apartment. Edmund and Boy watched him go down to the second terrace to retrieve the cart from Hiram.

"I'll be back this afternoon. We'll start then. Be ready!" Edmund warned. He grabbed a few books on a side shelf and left the apartment.

Boy sighed and plodded outside with the buckets, down the apartment stairs to the back steps. He looked into the gloomy shadows below, two hundred steps to the water. The wooden buckets were getting heavy already and they didn't yet have any water in them. Then he had an idea.

Boy dropped the buckets and ran to the carpenter's shop and told him what he wanted. He told the carpenter it was for Merl, so got no argument. *Well, it was for Merl, right? because Merl asked him to do it,* Boy rationalized. The carpenter was a good-natured man, with gnarled fingers and a hunched back from the work he did.

"How long have you been at the Arcanium," the carpenter asked.

36

"I arrived yestrday."

The carpenter gave him a knowing smile and nodded approvingly.

Boy couldn't figure out why the carpenter smiled at him. *What did that mean?* he wondered. Then Boy ran to the rope-winder and the cooper. He gathered from them all the supplies he could carry and returned to the apartment. The rope-winder also smiled at him in a similar way that Boy thought was meaningful, but didn't know the meaning.

Boy went back to the carpenter shop and picked up what he had ordered earlier, which because it was for the Merl, was finished.

When asked about money, he said, "It's for the Merl," and left the shop. He didn't stay to ask about the carpenter's mysterious smile.

Three hours later he had his contrivance finished. He had stretched a long rope with several buckets attached extending from the fountain at the bottom of the steps to the top of the steps. At the top end he attached a pulley and handle. When he turned the handle, empty buckets were dragged into the fountain basin, filled with water, and were dragged up the steps.. When they got to the top, Boy poured the water into his own two buckets and dumped the water into the bath tub.

After more than a dozen buckets, the tub was still not full. *How much water does this tub take?* he thought. *I'm glad I'm not walking up and down all those steps all day.* He was still pouring water when Edmund returned and saw the pulley

37

system.

"What are you doing?" Edmund asked.

"I've rigged up this system so that I can get the water in the tub faster but it doesn't seem to fill," Boy explained.

Edmund smiled sardonically. "I'm not surprised." He crooked a finger at Boy as he went inside. "Take a good look at that tub." He stood back and let Boy examine it.

Boy wasn't sure what he was suppose to do, but he examined the tub. It had a metal rim around the tub which was three feet deep, six feet long, and almost three feet wide; a large water reservoir for anyone. Then he noticed that a little bit of dust on the surface of the water was moving toward one side of the tub. He watched it disappear as it went under the curved rim. He stuck his finger underneath and felt a small oblong hole. The tub had an overflow drain! It would never get filled no matter how long he poured water into it. He imagined that if he had gone up and down those back steps, he would have been exhausted!

Was Merl punishing him for something? Oh, perhaps so! He almost broke his promise about keeping the ankigene secret this morning before Merl left. It seemed that even Edmund was not to know about that. Thinking back, he realized that *he* was not suppose to know about it either. If Edmund didn't know, then Merl must be entrusting Boy with a great and important secret. Yes, important enough to warn the King about it.

"Okay, you can stop now," Edmund said. "Let's check out your reading."

Edmund grabbed a book from one of the shelves and went outside to the porch. Boy and Edmund sat down together. Edmund surprisingly turned out to be a patient and focused teacher. Boy had little reason to read, living on the streets as he had, but he did read moderately well. Edmund walked Boy over the rough words and explained clearly whenever Boy had questions.

When they finished the reading lesson, Merl had not yet returned. Edmund pointed to the ropes and bucket contraption. "Take all that back to the craftsmen."

"What? We may want to fill up the tub again," Boy protested.

Edmund nodded his head. "Let me show you something." He stood and walked into the apartment. Boy followed. Edmund reached to the other side of the wall that the tub was against and Boy heard a Thunk! Water flowed into the tub, swirling and spinning and he could hear it gurgling out the overflow slot. "It was a test, Boy," Edmund explained.

"All that work for nothing?" Boy was angry that he had been manipulated.

"No, not for nothing. It was a test. You did well. In fact, I have never known someone to build a water delivery system on their first day. I'll tell Merl so when he returns.

At first, Boy simmered in anger as he pulled the ropes and buckets apart and piled them together but then he cooled when thinking about Edmund's praise. He felt proud that Edmund was going to pass along his good work.

Boy returned the ropes to the rope-winder, the buckets to the cooper, and the wooden pulleys and handle to the carpenter. The carpenter smiled and asked, "Did you do it? Did you finish the task today?"

"You knew about this?" Boy asked in surprise. "Couldn't you have told me?"

"Of course, but no. Merl always gives this test to newcomers," the carpenter replied. "But I couldn't tell you. It's Merl's test."

First Lesson

Four weeks passed uneventfully but then something unexpected happened: Merl decided to teach Boy about magic.

"Boy," Merl said one morning. "You showed initiative and intelligence in building that water delivery system. Many boys your age would not have thought of it. They would have broken their backs running up and down those stairs until they collapsed. Or worse, they would have given up and made up excuses for when I returned."

Boy swelled with pride.

"Also, Edmund tells me that you are a fair reader and a fast learner. I think today we will see what you can do with magic."

"What? You mean you will teach me magic?" Boy was surprised, especially since Merl had said Boy was not eligible to learn magic.

"We'll see" was all Merl would say.

"I can learn magic!" Boy was hopping with excitement. "Someday can I become Merl of the Academy? I want to become Merl."

"Hmph!" Merl scoffed. "That's the last thing we need, a little merl," he said dead-panned.

They walked together to the Library. "Morning, Merl" the Librarian said from behind the circular counter. Boy thought about what it would feel like to say "Good morning" back, as if he was the Merl.

"Morning, Haggard," Merl replied. "Is the Chamber available for an hour?"

Haggard checked a list under the counter. "Yes, yes it is." He replied. "When do you want it."

"Now, if it's no trouble."

Haggard reached under the counter and pulled out a ring of keys on which was a large brass key and two smaller ones. They looked ornate and old. He handed the key ring to Merl. "I'll mark you down," Haggard said, putting the list on the counter and writing something on it.

Boy was anxious to know what those ancient keys unlocked.

Merl took the keys. "Come," he said. As he walked, he talked. "See all those books? Most of them were not written by anyone in the Arcanium. They were written by a lost civilization hundreds of years ago. No one knows anything about that civilization except they appeared at the same time magic came into the world. The people who received the books treated the authors like gods.

41

"Gods gave magic to the world?" Boy asked.

"I don't think they were gods but they did know a lot at that time. They connected magic to the world with what's in those books." Merl paused in the center of the Library. "Some are incantations, which use sound to perform magic. Some are recipes for potions and some are rules for how to write magic spells onto scrolls or into books. It's no easy feat that." Merl continued walking along the Library.

Merl reached out and a book slid from the shelf four feet away and into his hand. He opened it. "See here." He turned to show the open pages to Boy.

Boy looked down and saw nothing he could read. Squiggles and swirls and little twisted marks. They were written in gold lettering...and wait! They were *glowing* slightly!

"Someday you might be able to read this," Merl said, sliding the book through the air back to its proper place on the shelf.

"You mean you'll teach me how to read magic?" Boy was ecstatic.

"We'll see," Merl replied again. Merl continued his lecture. "There are rules for how to perform magic and how to perform it without it going wrong." He paused. "Hmm. I've always wondered how many potential magicians have been lost in spells that backfired. That's why we are going to test you with something simple today."

Potential magicians that were lost in spells that backfired? Was

he going to do something dangerous? Boy was glad they were
going to start with something simple.

Merl walked to the far end of the huge library with
Boy right behind him. They stood before a blank rock wall
except for a keyhole to the left side. Merl shoved the large
key into the keyhole with a clank and turned. A grinding
screech was followed by a low rumbling as the rock wall
slid to the right, leading to a dark room on the other side
of the archway.

Merl entered and waved his arm from left to right. All
along the walls, candles lit up. The rock door slid shut. Boy
saw that they were in a cavernous room. he could see
various kinds of shelves of metal and wood along the
walls.

"Stay," Merl said. He walked into an alcove made by
two shelves and pulled a small cart with a plank of five
candles on it into the center of the room. He snapped his
fingers and the center candle lit. He then walked back to
Boy.

Merl looked at the boy. "Okay," he said slowly. "Blow
out the candle."

"What?" Boy didn't understand. "Just blow it out?"
He looked at the candle. He started to walk toward it.

Merl put a hand out to stop him. "No, from here."

"I don't think I can without getting closer."

"Clear your mind and imagine it happening. Imagine a
big gust of air blowing out the candle."

Boy thought this was a trick. *I am not going to be able to
blow out the candle from this distance. It must be ten feet away!* He

43

guessed that Merl would say, "Well, we tried." and that would be the end of that. No magic for Boy. "But..."

"Never mind the buts. Imagine a gust of wind traveling from your mind to the candle big enough to extinguish it."

Boy felt utterly disappointed, but he would try anyway. He concentrated on the candle until he was aware of nothing in the room except him and the candle. In his mind, he forced a big puff of air to cross the distance to the cart and *poof!* out went the candle. He straightened up and looked again: the candle was a lit as ever.

"It's a trick," Boy said sullenly. "I can't put that out with my mind."

"Try it again, but this time, say *Sarga* when you push the air."

Boy was suspicious. "*Sarga?*" He imagined again pushing a gust of air to the candle. As he did so, he said *Sarga.* Did he imagine it or did the candle flicker?

"Make the 's' softer and the 'g' harder, almost like *ssarka* and try a little harder in your mind."

Boy tried it again. "*Sarga!*" He blew out the word as he mentally blew out the candle. This time he could see the air waver and the candle definitely flickered.

"You have to have confidence that you can do it," Merl admonished. "Do you know you can extinguish the candle?"

"Yes, I think I can."

"No, you have to *know* you can."

Boy stood upright, crossed his arms, and thought

44

about that. *What did he know that he could definitely do? If he could borrow that conviction, then he might succeed.*

This time Boy visualized the candle directly in front of him instead of ten feet away on the cart. He imagined that he blasted air out and the candle went out—in his mind. He kept that image and puffed out *"Sarga!"* Air left his lips and grew into a transparent wavy ball that hit the candle. It went out! He blinked to see if it was really out or was he still imagining it. Yes, the candle was out! A small thin thread of smoke rose above the wick.

"Very good," Merl said, nodding his head. Merl had Boy extinguish the candle several more times for practice, each time moving the candle cart farther away.

In the last attempt, Merl lit all five candles with the cart thirty feet across the room. Boy imagined the air ball splitting into five as he exhaled *Sarga.* All five candles left smoke trails rising to the ceiling.

Merl stood wide-eyed. "That's the first time I've seen a student succeed on the first attempt. You have some powerful magic within you. Latent magic, but it's there."

Boy was surprised at himself. "Let's do more!"

"No. That's enough air magic. Let's try fire magic."

Fire magic? That sounded even better to Boy, but it also sounded more dangerous. However, he was basking in his glory. He could do anything—he thought. "Sure, let's do it."

Merl brought the cart back to Boy and stopped it five feet away. "Ok, you blew out those candles. Good. Now light them again."

45

What? How could he do that? Would a puff of air light a candle? No, that was for extinguishing candles. He tried the same trick as before. He concentrated in his mind on a small ball of fire going to the center candle and lighting it. Nothing happened. He blinked. "Should I have said *Sarga?*"

"No," Merl replied. "For this, say *Zocayati*".

"Say what?"

"*Zocayati.*" Merl spoke slower. "*zoko-YAtee.*"

Boy concentrated again, pictured small fireballs in his mind. He spat out *Zocayati* as he mentally thrust fireballs at the center candle. Nothing happened. No flicker, no light, no fire. His pride at his previous successes with air magic deflated. He couldn't do this part at all.

He tried again and again. After fifteen minutes of differing ways of imagining the center candle producing a flame, Merl said, "Okay, let's try something different."

At the end of two hours, Merl knew the Boy had an impressive talent for air magic and a good talent for water magic, but not much for fire magic and earth magic. Boy knew that too. Despite the coolness of the room, Boy was perspiring from the effort, and a small headache was forming at the base of his spine.

Boy also learned that there were other kinds of magic, like magic to make illusions, magic to transform one thing to another, and magic that played with peoples' minds. It was not for several years before Boy learned about black magic and necromancy, but that is a different story.

"I would like to try some animal magic with you," Merl said. "because it is one of the rarest and most useful kinds of magic. I always look for that in a new student, but we can do that later. And we don't have any animals here in the Library anyway," he added with a smile.

As Merl and Boy left the Library, Merl said, "Boy, wait in the hall a minute. I have something to discuss with Haggard. I'll be right out."

New student! He called me a new student! I am a student! Boy was elated over this new insight, perhaps a slip of tongue on Merl's part.

Then he thought about what Haggard and Merl might be discussing, but he remembered his talk—and his promise—on the first day after disobeying Merl, when Merl and Vulcan the blacksmith talked about ankigene.

Boy didn't stop to eavesdrop but he listened hard as he walked to the hallway. He heard Merl ask Haggard, "I was wondering if you can let Boy use the Chamber a little without me, when it is not in use, of course. He will practice..." and his voice trailed off as Boy left the room.

After that day, Boy came to the Chamber as frequently as he could and practiced different exercises that Merl suggested. He worked until he did them better than Merl had told him to expect. He thrilled to learn more about magic. Boy felt like a real student, although unofficial. Merl told him not to announce himself as a student if he wanted to continue working magic.

First Quake

Amidst cleaning and running errands for Merl, Boy

47

concentrated on his magic as often as he could. He loved it. Edmund began to teach him how to read the magic books. He thought the new language was easy and soon, he, Edmund, and Merl began to speak in the arcane language whenever they could.

Boy became close to Haggard, who recognized the boy's potential, and they often conversed in *arcanispeak*, which Haggard called the magic language. No one knew what the language was actually called, so that name was as good as any other.

One day Boy was returning a book and a scroll for Edmund and talking to Haggard when the earth began to shake and books tumbled from the shelves.

"Is someone in the Chamber?" Boy asked.

Haggard's eyes widened. "No, it's empty." Tables in the Library slid about and more books and scrolls fell to the floor.

"What's going on?" Boy gasped.

"I don't know." What seemed like a missile shot through the floor, narrowly missing Haggard, and stuck itself in the ceiling. It wobbled, then fell to the floor near Boy. It was a cylindrical sharply-pointed piece of black stone. A reddish glow throbbed at its center. Boy stared at it. He had seen this before. *Ankigene!* Then another piece flew through the floor and into the wall.

"Let's get out of here," Boy said.

"No, I'm staying with my books." Haggard swirled both hands over his head and down inside the counter space. A translucent greenish spherical shield enclosed him. He expected that his magical shield could protect him from the ankigene and debris flying about the Library. Boy was not so sure but he hoped that it would.

Boy heard screaming as the girls emptied the dormitory across the hall. Boy ran through the Library door and followed the panicked girls to the exit. A few of the older girls tried spells of protection and a few tried organizing the other girls to turn down the panic.

Soon he was in the plaza outside, where mobs of arcane students and magicians gathered. Some statues around the plaza had tumbled to the ground, a few broke into large pieces. Some of the stone buildings around the plaza dropped to the ground, making a loud rumble. A crack along the earth made a line of apple trees tilt dangerously close to falling over. Gorbal held his head and shook it back and forth. "Me trees! Me trees!" he cried.

Ankigene missiles flew from the earth with a high-pitched whistling as they shot high into the sky. Some landed back in the plaza causing people to rush for cover. Some landed far out toward Thentis.

In a few minutes, the quake was over and ankigene ceased firing into the sky. Merl stood outside his apartment and raised his hands. "People, people! It's all over. Count yourselves. Who is hurt? Is anyone missing?"

This small task occupied their minds and calmed the people somewhat. The professors took charge of organizing their classes and soon they moved back indoors in an orderly fashion, stepping around the debris.

Merl summoned the Boy below him in the plaza. By

49

the time Boy got to the porch, Merl was holding a black bag. It shimmered in his hand. Boy noticed that the bag was integrated with silver thread. Merl gave him the bag and said, "Pick up whatever pieces of ankigene you can find and put them in this bag. If anyone asks what you are doing, ask them to help you."

"Everything in the plaza?"

"Everything in the plaza and in any building. Check the craftsmen terraces where Vulcan and Hiram are too." Merl paused. "Except the girls dormitory. I'll get someone else for that."

Boy understood about the ankigene but he didn't understand the bag. *Was it special? Did it suppress any magic qualities that the ankigene might have? How can ankigene blast from the earth like it did? Was he in danger carrying a bag of ankigene around with him? What if it exploded?*

Boy ran down to the plaza and quickly but carefully moved pieces of ankigene into the bag. The pieces were of different sizes but they were all shaped about the same— long black pointed cylinders and they all had a glowing red center.

He cleared the plaza, then cleared the terraces, Library, and hallways. He was glad to see that Haggard was safe and no longer within his protective sphere.

When Boy returned to the plaza, some people were lying on the ground, some sitting on whatever they could find. A few brown-robe clerical healers moved from person to person. They were not members of the Arcaneum, so they must have come up from Thentis. That idea was confirmed when he saw the soldiers.

Boy saw several armed guards dressed in the official Thentian soldier colors of orange and red. Some were checking on people's injuries, some were lifting fallen statues back into place. After seeing students in dull-colored clothing and professors in grey robes for so long, the soldiers looked out of place. They didn't fit in with the silver and marble ambience of the Arcaneum.

One burly soldier's orange and red uniform had black embossing. He talked with Merl near the door of Merl's apartment. Boy was too far away to hear what they were saying, but from appearances, this soldier was in charge.

First Test

Fortunately, there were no deaths or serious injuries from the quake, only minor sprains and a couple broken bones. The clerics were able to administer successfully to some injuries and magically heal other injuries; time was needed for others.

Still, some students and two professors decided to leave the Arcaneum as being too dangerous. Classes were canceled temporarily. Everyone that stayed spent their time repairing and reorganizing the Arcaneum.

After order was restored a few days later, Merl came to Boy.

"Boy, you have studied long and hard," Merl said, "and your skills almost match Edmund's, even though he still knows a lot more than you. I think it is time we took a trip together, get you some *practical* experience."

Boy was going with Merl somewhere? It must be a quest. "Certainly. I would love to do that. Where are we going?"

"To the other side of the mountain to deal with this ankigene. Can't have it lying about all the time."

"What *is* ankigene?" Boy asked. "I've never seen rocks fly out of the ground before."

"Let's hope you never have to again." Merl sat on the steps outside his apartment. "I guess you may as well know. You'll probably find out about it soon enough, with all the time you spend in the Library." He smiled.

"Every Arcaneum that we know about was eventually destroyed by ankigene quakes," Merl began. "This last quake was not catastrophic but it could have been."

Boy picked up his head to look at Merl. "There are other Arcaneums?" Boy asked.

"Of course there are, or were. The larger ones are gone. We are the largest left, although a few cloisters still exist in small areas around the kingdom."

"Where does ankigene come from?" Boy asked.

"We don't know." Merl answered. "We know it has something to do with magic but not how. One prevailing theory is that it was once regular rock that converted to ankigene after a long time exposed to the magic fields used by the larger Arcaneums. After all, we have a lot of people practicing magic here in one spot." Merl paused to let that sink in.

"Magic fields?" Boy asked.

"Yes, whenever one does magic, a special kind of field is set up in the area," Merl replied. "Fields are of different shapes. Your air magic creates long thin fields, like one might imagine a wind to be. Fire magic sets up spherical fields, and so on. These fields allow some spells to work, like *Detect Magic* or *Illusion* spells."

"With all the different kinds of magic used in the Arcaneum," he continued, "the rocks of the mountain undergo a transformation. Some say these magic fields *create* the ankigene over time."

"So we, I mean, those who study magic here at the Arcaneum, caused the ankigene...and the quake?" Boy asked.

Merl shrugged. "Alternatively," he said, "perhaps it is ankigene that allows the Arcaneums to perform magic. Magic does have a preference as to where it works best. The ankigene is like an ore that enables magic, which is why Arcaniums exist where they do."

Merl fell into thought and stared out over the long steps down to Thentis. He was quiet for several minutes. Boy waited patiently.

"A friend of mine, a man named Gregorio, knows a lot about rocks," Merl continued. "We are going to take these bags of ankigene to him. Let him study them for awhile and see what he finds out."

"Is that dangerous?" Boy wondered. "Can they explode on the trip?"

Merl laughed. "No, they're perfectly safe. They're just rocks, but a special kind of rock. We'll be fine."

53

He stood up. "We leave tomorrow at dawn, so be ready."

Ankigene was related to magic! Boy wondered: *how so? Did ankigene make magic stronger? Did it stop magic? Could it be used with magic, perhaps as a protection?* Boy waited until Edmund and Merl were elsewhere and picked a piece of ankigene from one of the silver bags, a small piece about an inch in diameter and three inches long that he hoped would not be missed.

He took Merl's spare nazulwood walking stick. Most professors carried nazulwood walking sticks because nazulwood was thought to focus their magic energies better. Boy had never used one before, even for walking. He thought about what Merl had said about magic fields. He imagined that perhaps nazulwood aligned magic fields, which is why they made magic stronger.

He pushed the ankigene into his pocket and rushed to the Library Chamber to test his idea. Once inside, he put the ankigene and the walking stick on the floor near the door. He wondered what kind of magic he should use to test ankigene. It had a red center, so he thought *fire magic*, but fire magic was one of his worst skills. Well, he would try that first and if nothing happened, he'd try something else.

Boy went to the far side of the Chamber and pushed the candle cart to the center of the far wall. He had successfully practiced fire magic before, but was rewarded with only a small and disappointing result.

He stood back ten feet from the candle cart and tried

to light the center candle. He mentally pushed a small fireball at the candle. The center candle lit. Then he used his air magic to extinguish the flame and tried to light three candles. He lit three candles on the second try. *Okay*, he thought, *That's about all I can do by myself. Now for the ankigene.*

He retrieved the nazulwood walking stick from near the door and returned to the candle cart. He pointed the stick and pushed fire from his mind along the stick. Three candles lit on the first try! *Well, that's something,* Boy thought. He used the stick to blow out the candles. He noticed that he didn't have to concentrate as hard for air magic when he focused with the nazulwood.

Now for the real test. He retrieved the ankigene from near the door. He didn't want to have ankigene in his hand when he attempted any magic. Who knows what could happen? Perhaps nothing, but perhaps it would burn his hand, or shoot into the ceiling like before, or maybe explode.

He tied the ankigene firmly to the end of the walking stick for safety. He stood back ten feet and took cover around one tall cabinet. He wanted *some* protection in case the ankigene exploded. He tentatively stuck the stick out from behind the cabinet.

He wanted to push his fire energy into the ankigene at the end of the stick and onto the candles in the cart. He hesitated. *What if it blew up, or backfired and put him on fire?* He hesitated. *Well, this is getting me nowhere.* He had to do something.

"Let's do it!" he said aloud. He concentrated his fire

magic along the stick. Because he was weak at this skill, he concentrated hard and pushed hard. He tried to light the center candle again.

This time, the red glow of the ankigene grew and grew until the entire piece glowed a bright red. The entire Chamber was bathed in red light. The glow shot out from the end of the nazulwood in a fireball that blasted the cart. It didn't light the candles: it melted them and caught the wooden cart on fire! The fireball carried on past the now-burning cart and dissipated when it hit the Chamber wall.

Boy was stunned. His legs weakened and he shook in shock. He collapsed to the ground on his butt, unable to hold himself upright. *What had he found?*

He realized that not only did the nazulwood and ankigene magnify his magic, it *drained* it from him more than he intended. He started the magic by pushing with his mind, but soon, the magic was pulled from inside him. *Could a powerful spell exhaust him as the ankigene drew his energy from him?*

He saw the burning cart. He didn't know what Haggard would think of this. He stood and pointed the staff at it and threw his air magic to put out the cart. From the end of the staff, the ball of air extinguished the flames and pushed the cart sideways, closer to the wall. He felt his power leave him, like someone twisting his innards as they pulled them out. He leaned against one of the shelves for support, barely able to stand. He was in awe at the power he wielded. *Could it pull his magic enough to kill him?*

Quickly he packed his stuff and left the Chamber. On

the way out, as he passed the checkout counter, he threw Haggard a quick "You need to replace the candles." Then he was out the door, and out of range of the Librarian who might ask embarrassing questions.

What to do with this knowledge? Ankigene multiplied magic forces! Perhaps it needed nazulwood to do that, perhaps not. Merl was about to remove two bags of ankigene that the Arcaneum might be able to use. He decided to tell Merl about it.

After Merl's initial disbelief, Merl decided to try a similar experiment. Merl pulled a small piece of ankigene from one of the bags. It was slightly larger than Boy's piece but he attached it to his walking stick. Both Boy and Merl entered the Chamber. Haggard had not been in the Chamber since Boy left so the candle cart sat against the far wall, still smouldering.

Merl looked at Boy, then raised his staff. A blinding light shot from his staff and illuminated the entire usually gloomy Chamber. Merl frowned and the light grew dimmer. Merl smiled.

He tilted his head and a flame shot from the staff and hit the ceiling in a roiling flame 20 feet long. Burnable items near the flame in the Chamber began to blacken and scorch. He changed his grip on the staff and the flame was replaced with a water fountain and drenched everything in the room. Then the fountain drooped into a drizzle. Merl and Boy were drenched but Merl was laughing.

"This is extraordinary!" Merl laughed with glee. "We can control this. It is not an all-or-nothing effect," he said almost to himself. "I was a bit premature in wanting to give Gregorio all that ankigene. We'll give him some and keep a few pieces here for our own experiments."

Boy noticed that this was the first time that Merl had referred to him and Merl as "we".

"Didn't anyone ever try ankigene and nazulwood together?" Boy asked. "Now that we have, it seems obvious that the two would amplify magic."

"Not that I know," Merl answered. "I guess we have been so careful about keeping it secret because of the dangers, we never tried to learn much about it. But now, I'll certainly look into it."

First Quest

Boy and Merl started out slightly after dawn. Each carried one of the silver bags loaded with ankigene. Merl had pulled out what he thought was sufficient for the Arcaneum professors to use. Both he and Boy carried their walking staves tipped with ankigene, which now were truly *magic staves*. They stepped lightly as they descended the 200-step back stairway toward the fountain.

Merl told Boy how to open the secret back door. With pride, Boy opened and closed it magically. They made their way along a trail that wrapped around the mountain. Their plan was to reach Gregorio that evening, stay overnight and discuss the ankigene and its unexpected properties with him, and return the following day.

They walked along a narrow trail that ran along the

mountain. A steep cliff rose to their right and a steep cliff fell away on their left. The trail was wide enough for a horse-drawn cart of goods, or for three horses to stand side-by-side, as they soon found out. Boy looked over the edge. He could see the rooftops of a small village in the distance far below.

"We are really high!" Boy exclaimed.

Then they heard hoofbeats as a group of mounted marauders came upon them. The leader signaled for the bandits to stop. "Well, lookee what we have here," he said. "Some travelers that are using our road."

The leader turned to Merl. "Where are you heading? Have you paid your road tax?" he asked smugly.

Merl knew there was no road tax but he replied, "We are poor travelers heading for the town of Mystic Woods. We are visiting a friend."

"You still need to pay your road tax." He leaned on his saddle and smiled, "Tell you what: since you are a long way from home, we'll do you a favor. We'll collect your tax and see to it that it gets to the tax collector." The men laughed and nodded their heads. "Yeah, the tax collector."

"But we have nothing of value to you," Merl replied.

"I see that you are carrying something in those silvery bags. Must be valuable if they are in there."

"Only rocks." Merl put down his bag and pulled out a piece of ankigene to demonstrate. He was careful to keep his hand over the red glow at the center lest its unusualness pique the bandits' attention.

"Only rocks, eh?" the leader asked incredulously.

59

"Who carries rocks around? They must be special rocks indeed for you to go to all that trouble. I think we'll take those rocks. And while we're at it, we'll take whatever else we want."

He gestured with a twist of his hand and the horsemen lifted loaded crossbows and aimed them at Merl and Boy. "Hand them over!" the leader demanded.

"Hmm," Merl said. "I think we won't do that, but I know what you will do. You will think about how rash it is to attack strangers, think about it all the way down."

"Way down? We're not going anywhere, but you are. You are going to your death if you don't hand over your goods!" Two of the crossbowmen fired their bolts at Merl, another one fired at Boy.

Merl circled his hand, palm out, and muttered something. The bolts bounced off an invisible wall in front of him with two dull thuds. Boy did the same, since he had learned a thing or two from the Arcaneum after all. The third arrow thudded into his barrier then fell to the ground.

"Now it's our turn." Merl replied angrily. "*Periplu!*" he shouted, circling his staff at the bandits. A transparent sphere of wavy air surrounded the bandits and their horses, which then floated a foot above the ground.

The men's eyes widened and they shouted in surprise. "Argh!" The remaining men with loaded crossbows fired them. The bolts passed through the levitation sphere, but not through Merl's protective shield. The leader jumped from this horse but did not land on the ground as he had hoped. His feet stood even with the hooves of his horse above the ground.

Merl turned to Boy. "Now your turn. But not fire, air will be sufficient. A small push, I think." Merl smiled.

The men listened to this exchange in alarm, not comprehending what the old man meant.

Boy smiled. He raised his staff and the bandits cowered in their saddles. "*Sarga!*" A blast of wind roared from his staff. The wind moved the levitation sphere off the trail and out over thin air, including the entire squad of terrified men.

They were no longer on the mountain trail. They looked down. One tried to jump from his horse and gain the ledge along the trail, but he bounced off the side of the sphere and slide to the bottom. The bandits were too far off the trail, but they didn't fall. The horses, white-eyed and shrieking, reared and stomped about, threatening the two men at the bottom the sphere.

Slowly, the levitation sphere descended with the bandits and horses inside until they were out of sight below the trail. The shouts of the men and horses diminished as they descended.

Merl chuckled, "They will take about twenty minutes to descend to Shakleford's Mill below. That'll give them plenty of time to think about attacking strangers. I don't think they will be in the mood to raid people down there." He pursed his lips. "It's a shame. They could do so much good if they only *tried* to do good."

After a moment, Boy said, "Merl, why couldn't they

61

get out of the sphere but the crossbow bolts almost shot us?"

"The levitation sphere only works on living things. I don't know why, but that's how the magic works." Merl frowned slightly. "There is a lot about magic that we don't understand. Perhaps that's where you can help out, little merl." Merl smiled. Boy thought about what he could do to improve magic, or people's knowledge of magic.

They arrived at a mid-sized town about dusk, as planned. They wandered through main streets and side streets until they found Gregorio's house. Gregorio and Merl were happy to see each other again.

Every table, bench, and mantel in every room in the house that Boy could see was covered with rocks of different sizes, shapes, and colors.

Gregorio took a couple ankigene pieces in his hands. "When ankigene changes, for whatever reason," he said, "it splits the bedrock into these similarly shaped fragments. Why they shoot out of the earth afterwards is a puzzle no one knows the answer to. At least I don't. That's why I would love to study them."

During dinner they learned that Gregorio knew little about ankigene. He knew that it started as underlying bedrock that changed with time. Ankigene was rare and only appeared in certain places. Merl had told Boy that ankigene appeared under Arcaneums but Gregorio seemed not to know about that and Merl didn't mention it. In fact, Merl didn't mention magic at all. Boy decided to keep quiet about magic too, and what they had learned yesterday in the Chamber.

The rest of the meal and evening were uneventful. Boy had hoped that Gregorio might let slip Merl's real name but no such luck. Gregorio called him only Merl during the entire visit. The next morning, Boy and Merl left to return home.

On the way, about the same place where they had encountered the bandits the day before, they encountered the bandits again. The bandits rode around the corner and saw them. They pulled their horses up short. The leader shouted, "It's them!" Boy wondered if they would try to get revenge and attack, but instead, they turned and fled.

Boy relaxed. "Well, they learned something from yesterday."

"I'm not so sure. They are still on patrol for victims," Merl said. They never saw the bandits the rest of the day.

Last Quake

Boy and Merl had many adventures over the next several months. Boy learned much about magic of all kinds but neither Boy nor Merl learned much more about ankigene.

Another ankigene quake hit the Arcaneum and this one was much worse than the last. After it subsided, Merl called for a general evacuation of the Arcaneum to save as many people as he could.

Gorbal packed up his tree seedlings into a cart and pulled it down the long steps to Thentis. Vulcan gathered

63

his forge and blacksmith tools. Hiram led his cart teams of horses and donkeys from his terrace down to Thentis. The remaining brave professors and students who had stayed after the first quake evacuated after Merl encouraged them to leave.

Only Haggard, Edmund, Merl, and Boy stayed behind to protect the invaluable Library from destruction. Each was armed with ankigene-nazulwood magic staves, which by now had become common for most of the school magicians.

When the last catastrophic quake came, the earth cracked open and buildings fell in stone avalanches. Haggard and Edmund gathered to save the Library, the last bastion of magical writings. It seemed the densest concentration of ankigene missiles occurred in the Library.

Haggard and Edmund shielded themselves and magically supported shelves and scrolls as the walls around them collapsed. They shot missiles of air and fire to divert the falling ceiling. They put up walls of protections over many of the books and themselves. Still, fallen slabs of stone fell over many of the books, which were then ironically protected from other falling rocks.

Merl and Boy joined to mitigate much of the destruction. Ankigene missiles continued to shoot into the ceiling, causing great slabs of rock to fall. Since they couldn't stop the destruction, they tried to redirect the falling rock to form a wall around the books and scrolls, and leave a path through it.

It seemed the ankigene missiles would never stop.

Eventually Edmund and Haggard, who had been in the Library fighting longer, were exhausted both physically and magically. Haggard's green spherical protective shell flickered and went out. His protection walls dimmed and disappeared. Haggard leaned against the counter, breathing heavily.

Edmund saw a slab of rock falling directly toward Haggard. Edmund jumped closer to Haggard and tried to blast the rock to smithereens, but his magic was too weak. The slab of rock continued to fall downward on the two magicians.

Boy saw it too. He tried to move the falling rock away from Haggard and Edmund, but it was too little too late. A piece of ceiling fell with a crash on both Edmund and Haggard, who disappeared beneath the rock and dust.

Boy stood staring at the loss of his two friends.

"Move, Boy!" Merl shouted. He pulled Boy backward toward the hallway door. Another piece of rock barely missed falling on Boy.

A few more ankigene missiles exploded from the Library floor. Boy and Merl were forced from the Library into the hallway. Boy noticed the door to the girls' dormitory had collapsed. Then the ankigene missiles stopped.

Boy and Merl stared at the destruction in the Library. Boy said nothing, but he realized that they had succeeded in keeping most of the magical resources accessible. A ragged path lead from the hallway to the Chamber beyond.

"They died a valiant death," Merl said, leaning against

his staff as he stared into the dust and rubble. "They helped save what may be left of magic in the world. They will be missed."

Boy was too exhausted and overwhelmed to say anything. Soon they moved tiredly to the plaza outside, now covered in boulders strewn about like bushes in a meadow. Statues were down and broken. The apple trees were smashed by stone or had fallen into large crevasses in the earth.

Boy was dismayed when he saw the plaza totally destroyed. He climbed the stairs to the porch in front of Merl's apartment, winding his way around fallen rock. He could see that the tunnel of 200 steps to the back door fountain was still passable. He returned to Merl, who was using earth magic to clear a passageway through the debris.

Last Wizard

More ankigene blasted from the earth again. The barrage of lethal missiles from the ground and crushing rock from above started all over. This time, the accompanying earthquake was worse. The buildings shook, and crevasses opened in the floor.

Thentian soldiers had come running when the first quake started but now it was too late for this second quake. There was nothing they could do. Merl, Boy, and the soldiers struggled to keep their footing as the ground shook beneath them. They all evacuated slowly to the top of the stairs that led back to Thentis.

Boy and Merl fought back to back, magically diverting falling rock to protect themselves and the retreating soldiers. Boy didn't know how much longer he could hold his staff up; his arms burned with exertion. He felt hollow inside from the magic power being pulled from him. He didn't know much magic he had left in him.

Is it my imagination or does the ankigene follow the Merl? Boy wondered. *It always seems to be heaviest wherever the Merl is.* It didn't occur to Boy that perhaps the ankigene followed them both as they wielded their magic.

One of the walls broke off from a tall building and started to fall inward to the plaza directly above Boy and Merl. Merl pushed Boy aside but Merl couldn't avoid it. The wall fell on Merl, crushing him.

Boy and the soldiers tried to lift off the slab of rock on top of Merl, but in vain. Boy tried to help magically but he was not strong enough. Merl was too weak to contribute.

Merl, covered in dust and bits of rock, waved his only good arm to summon Boy closer. He groaned. "Boy, you must leave me. My time here is over," he whispered in a hoarse rasp, "but yours is beginning."

Boy brushed off the dust on Merl with his robe as best he could. "No. No. We can get you out of here." Boy objected. "We can get more soldiers—" Boy was interrupted as two tall buildings on either side of the plaza toppled toward each other, closing any entrance to Merl's apartment and the Library from the direction of Thentis. Anyone climbing the stairs now would only see the rockslide of a collapsed mountain.

Boy thought that maybe behind that impassable fallen wall, the Library, Merl's apartment, and the back fountain stairway were still passable, but not from here.

Merl coughed and spit up blood. "Our Arcaneum is no more. You have done all you can here, little merl. You have become more powerful than anyone else your age. You have the makings of a great wizard, a famous wizard. The Library is saved." Merl wheezed and coughed up more blood.

"You can use the back fountain door to get in to study whenever you need, to grow your power, or to take refuge from the world, which sometimes is necessary. Come here when you need but keep it secret."

"But...but--" Boy could think of nothing to say.

"Now listen," Merl was in earnest. He pulled Boy down with his one good arm. "There is a young boy, a royal in the north, someone who could change the world with your help. Go to him. Advise him. Teach him fairness and justice, that Might doesn't make Right." Merl coughed again. "Be wise and lead the world to a better place...little merl." Merl smiled and closed his eyes for the last time.

Boy rarely shed tears. They were a weakness when living on the street. He tried to hold back tears now. With a painful lump in his throat, he slowly left his dying mentor.

Captain Barak, leader of the Thentean soldiers asked one of his soldiers. "That young man is a strong magician. Who is he? What's his name?"

The soldier who had been close enough to have heard

the end of Merl's dying wish, said, "I think his name is Merlyn" he told Barak. "At least I think that's what Merl called him."

What Barak and the soldier did not understand was that Merl had spoken to Boy in *arcanispeak*. What the soldier overheard was "little chief" or "little merl" in that language: *merlyn*.

Barak stood sadly beside the boy, understanding some of his loss. Finally Barak asked, "Is your name Merlyn?"

Boy's thoughts were interrupted by this question. He had been thinking about Edmund, and Haggard, and all the other fine people he had known and lost. He thought about Merl and how he still didn't know Merl's given name.

Boy was about to say "No, I don't know my given name" but then stopped. *Merl called me "little merl, little chief" all the time.* Although Merl said it in jest, Boy realized that as inexperienced as he was, he was now the last representative of the Arcanium, the last wizard.

His thoughts returned to Barak's question. *What was his name? Merlyn was as a good a name as any*, he thought.

Out of respect for his magical mentor, he realized that he would keep that name.

"Yes," Boy said. "My name is Merlyn."

Plots from Literary Estates

Dream Stories

Sometimes writing out a story is a lot of work, rework, and revision. Other times a story comes to me "whole cloth", and I try to put it on paper as fast as I can. The stories in this category are called "dream stories" because they came directly from dreams I've had.

Most people's dreams are a collage of somewhat surreal images and actions, and some are scenes. The dreams that I've converted to stories came complete with plot, action, characters, and sometimes color. Go figure. I rack it up as a result of watching too many late night movies.

Each of these dream stories are short human dramas in contemporary, or near-contemporary, settings. They are a far cry from the fantasy adventures or stylistic experiments I usually write when I'm awake. Perhaps the stories say less about my dreams and more about who I am. I hope they do not reflect poorly on my subconscious self.

I am amazed that my own dreams could surprise me. How can that be when the entire idea comes from myself? It's like learning new information when one is talking to oneself.

The dream that led to the first story, *Stand Off*, started as a landscape, an eerie canvas of gray.

Then during the dream, I heard sounds, and I was back in old "Twilight Zone" episodes of World War II. The dream coalesced into what became the story. Like several others in this collection, the plot involves trickery. (Perhaps I am subconsciously a con artist.)

Stand Off is a World War II story played out mostly between two enemy soldiers. Thinking of the end as I woke, I thought, "What a neat trick!" I tried to relay the realism of the scene as best I could, having never been in a war.

The second story, *The Psychic*, is short, almost an anecdote, about a poor schmuck trying to hit on a pretty waitress. Again, I woke with the idea that a neat trick had been performed. It contains a twist ending which has its own twist ending. How does my brain come up with this stuff?

The next story, *The Fire*, was the hardest to write. Usually I prefer narrative action stories, but this one was loaded with emotion. I don't usually do emotion—or do it well. (The first time I tried, my family laughed at me after reading the drafts because it was so off-key.)

This story left me with a kaleidoscope of strong emotions. To write this story, I would have to transfer and emote in the reader these strong emotions by using subtext. And not just one, but several. If you are disturbed by this story, then I did my job.

I woke up angry after the dream that led to *Pecos Bay*, an anger based on an unjustified misunderstanding that quickly subsided and left me feeling stupid and embarrassed at myself. The dream, and subsequent story, stuck with me over the next several weeks. It was hard to push out of my mind. (The image of the girl in the green swimsuit on the hydroplane stuck with me a long time, like a color wallpaper image on my mind!)

Pecos Bay may have been influenced by the only hydroplane practice session that I attended about a month earlier. This story I had to get right. My writing had to be precise; to get that feeling of misunderstanding and anger, and to pass the resulting feeling of misunderstanding to the reader. I hope I succeeded.

If you don't like these stories, try not to judge me too harshly. After all, I was dreaming and didn't mean it.

Plots from Literary Estates

Stand Off

The battle was fought in a strip mine, and aerial bomb craters made it look worse. The entire scene was gray. A gray pit of gravel and gray cliffs with layers of rocky ledges on a gray cloudy day. Even the German soldier who wandered onto the scene was covered in gray dust, making him fit into the landscape in a surreal way.

That's what Sergeant McClusky of the U.S. Army saw when he peered over the rim of the crater-like strip mine. He kept low and out of sight of the German soldier.

Strangely, there were only two bodies on the floor of the mine. One was a German officer, gasping and moaning in pain near the inner edge of a deep depression partially filled with water. Another was an American officer, lying thirty feet from the German officer. He made no sound. He might have been mistaken for dead except that his chest slowly rose and fell with his shallow breathing.

"He's alive," the corpsman said, looking into the pit

through binoculars. "I can see him breathing."

Sergeant McClusky took the binoculars from the corpsman and confirmed. "We've got to get him out of there," he said.

"But how? HQ says German reinforcements will be here in twenty minutes, and you've got that soldier standing down there right now. We don't have any rifles, and I'm out of ammo."

McClusky checked his sidearm. "I have three rounds left."

"It would be suicide," the corpsman added.

McClusky looked down at the soldier, a German infantry private armed with a Karabiner K98, a powerful weapon, and an easy shot from down there.

McClusky's Colt 45 sidearm, although immensely powerful against a charging enemy at close range, would be widely inaccurate at this range. He pondered the problem, then he saw a glint in the nearby bushes. He had an idea.

A few minutes later McClusky pulled his Colt and lifted it above his head. He shouted down to the soldier in his barely adequate German.

"*Privat, nicht schiessen!* Private, don't shoot!"

The soldier was immediately on alert. He went to his knee and aimed his rifle directly at McClusky.

"*Nicht schiessen!*" the sergeant repeated.

"*Geben Sie sich auf?* Are you surrendering?" the soldier replied, sighting more carefully along the rifle's barrel.

"*Die Schlacht ist vorbei.* The battle's over," McClusky

76

said, "You want your man, and I want my man," McClusky continued in German. "There is no need to shoot." He waited to see how the infantryman responded. No change. "Can I come down and get my wounded man?" McClusky asked.

McClusky tried to size up the German soldier. He was light-haired and thin with a good face. He was young, very young. Too young for war, McClusky thought. The boy was probably patriotic when he joined the war. He joined for a noble cause like most boys hearing about the war. Then once in, it was too late. He learned the harsh realities of war. Like most naïve young soldiers, the veneer of idealism shattered and he realized he was in a nightmare world of blood, cruel violence, and unfair play. However, he was trapped. He didn't want to appear cowardly or unpatriotic. He could not renounce his earlier beliefs as wrong; he could barely face them. He wanted to take it all in stride, like his superiors and the facade of his fellow soldiers.

The young German soldier stood with rifle aimed. He saw the enemy not surrendering, but not attacking either. He licked his lips and said nothing. Should he shoot?

McClusky called out in his barely adequate German. "I want to rescue my wounded. You want to rescue your wounded. The longer we wait, the worse it is for them. Can I come down to get my man?"

Officers always seemed to know the right answers, particularly in situations such as this, but this one only groaned. He glanced over at the wounded officer. Blood trickled from beneath the officer's hand, clamped to his side. Blood spread across his uniform and trickled into the water, producing little eddies of red on the gray surface. Perhaps this Amerikaner had a plan that both could follow. Perhaps the agonizing groan from the wounded German officer in the watery crater helped the soldier-boy decide. The infantryman licked his lips again and then jerked his head in a quick nod.

"*Ich komme runter.* I'm coming down," McClusky said. He slowly slipped one leg over the rim and paused, seeing if the soldier would shoot. He didn't. McClusky put his other leg over the rim and stood on the steep slope of the strip mine. He was committed now.

"I'm going to put my gun away," McClusky said, still in German. He slowly put his sidearm into its holster on his belt. He kept his hands out, not above his head as if surrendering, but out to the side, as if he was being frisked to show that he was hiding nothing.

He half slid, half stumbled down the rocky side of the pit. He tried to avoid falling onto one of the grapefruit-size rocks but he didn't want to make any sudden moves in front of this boy with a deadly weapon either. He reached the bottom and took a deep breath, his hands still out at the side.

The boy soldier still aimed his gun at McClusky. Although he looked nervous, he held the gun steady and directly at the army sergeant. McClusky knew that the boy would not hesitate to shoot if it came to that.

McClusky took a deep breath. "If any shooting starts

down here now, the sniper on the rim will take you out."

The boy's eyes widened. He jerked his gaze around the rim. "*Ich sehe keinen Scharfschützen.* I don't see a sniper," the boy replied.

"Change your angle, or step over there. You should see the glint of the sniper scope or the end of the sniper's muzzle." McClusky let his hands slowly fall to his side.

The boy tried to cover McClusky with his rifle while he moved about and spot the sniper at the same time. His head and rifle pivoted jerkily. His K98 and eyes darted back and forth between the American threat in front of him and the one on the rim. Three feet farther from McClusky and the soldier froze. He paled. He slowly put his rifle over his head—surrender position.

"*Nein.* You don't need to surrender," McClusky said. "You get your man and I'll get mine." The sergeant moved closer to his man, Captain Meyers, a step at a time. The German soldier did the same, and they both moved in parallel to their wounded comrades.

McClusky nodded in consent and bent down to his captain, ready to jump aside if the boy decided to shoot. It was a tenuous thread that kept the German from shooting both him and Meyers. McClusky put Meyer's arm over his shoulder and pulled him up.

The German soldier wanted to do the same, but he held his Karabiner rifle, still aimed at McClusky. He couldn't pick up his wounded man while still holding his weapon. The boy thought about it, then decided. He slung his rifle across his back by the strap and lifted the wounded German officer to his feet. The officer grunted in pain but got his feet under him. He was only partially conscious.

Both the American and German pairs hobbled back to where they first encountered each other on the embattled floor. The boy's mouth tightened into a straight line, an acknowledgment that things worked out, perhaps thankful that he had not been sniper shot. Perhaps thankful for a shred of humanity in this hellish world. The boy walked to the east, away from McClusky, and guided the almost-walking officer from the battle scene.

The sergeant slung his unconscious captain over his shoulders and moved strenuously up to the rim of the mine. The corpsman threw down a length of rope to help lift the captain the last several feet.

Once at the top, both men put Captain Meyers on an impromptu litter. McClusky took one last look over the rim. The German soldier and his officer were gone. McClusky moved a dozen feet along the rim and lifted a discarded green beer bottle from the ground, one he had carefully positioned before going over the crater edge toward the German soldier. He showed the beer bottle to the corpsman and smiled. The corpsman grinned broadly. The idea had worked!

The sergeant threw the beer bottle into the brush. A beer bottle with the greenish color of a tinted sniper scope. A beer bottle with a long neck that could be confused at a distance for the shape and length of a sniper muzzle protruding over the top of the dirt ridge.

The Psychic

Tall, dark, and handsome pushed the door open to the small diner and entered just after the daily lunch rush. He walked casually to a booth and settled into it. The waitress, a delightful beauty as fresh as a Georgia peach, came up to serve him.

"What can I get you, honey?" she said.

He looked up, saw her, and smiled.

"Coffee, for now--" He looked at her name tag. "Wilma".

She returned the smile, added a note to her order pad, and left. She returned with a cup and a pot of coffee and poured it for him. She smiled. He smiled.

She returned several minutes later. "Anything?" she said to the stranger.

"No, I think not. Just coffee." he replied. He put a few dollar bills onto the table for the coffee and a tip. He looked up at her, "Did you know I'm a psychic?"

"Really," she replied, disbelief evident in her voice.

"Do you believe in psychics?"

"Well, maybe."

"I can prove it." He studied her angelic face for a moment. "I'm sensing that you have suffered loss in your family." He paused. "I'm getting a feeling, someone whose name starts with M?"

"No good," Wilma said with a wry grin. "Everyone has suffered loss, and almost everyone in these parts has a name of someone in their family that starts with M. Hmm. I don't think you can prove you're a psychic." She smoothly slid the bills into her serving apron and plunked down the receipt from the order pad onto the table. She turned away but then stopped. She turned back again.

"Perhaps there is a way you can prove it, if you're legit."

"Sure!" He smiled openly. "What do you have in mind?"

"Give me ten dollars." She stared at him, daring him to decline.

"Oh, ah…" His eyes shifted about the emptying diner. "Why?"

"To prove you are a psychic, like you claim."

"Ah, ok." He pulled a ten-dollar bill from his wallet and put it in front of her.

"Okay, good." She leaned over and spoke directly to him. "I'm going to go into the kitchen for a minute. When I return, I want you to tell me which pocket I put it in, Mr. Psychic."

Slowly a smile spread across his face. "Fine. Let's do it."

She held the bill up in front of his eyes, then above her head as she disappeared into the kitchen. Mr. Psychic had a few tense moments wondering about his ten dollars but she returned promptly.

"Ok, which pocket is the ten-dollar bill in?" she asked.

He smiled. "That's a trick question. It is not in your pocket. It is in your bra."

"Oh yes?"

"Women carry many things about with them," he explained, "but out of some evolutionary instinct, or some cultural habit, they put things in their bra for *extra* safekeeping. In order to win this little bet, you wanted me to be wrong. To be extra safe, you put it in your bra." He grinned smugly.

"Well, Mr. Psychic, your wrong. It is not in my bra, but I'm not going to take off my top for you to prove it."

"Can I get another guess?" he asked taken aback.

"Guess?" she said, "Psychics don't guess."

"It's in your left pocket," he said, tilting his head in that direction.

"Humph!" She pulled a ten-dollar bill from her right pocket. "Wrong again! I guess I don't believe you are a psychic." She turned and walked away.

"Wait!" he called back. "What about my ten dollars?"

She turned around and grinned devilishly, "That was the real test. I never said I would return the money to you. You didn't psych that out." She turned and flounced away.

His mouth dropped open as she left the area. He closed his mouth and left the diner.

Another server came on duty to start her shift. "How's the day been, Wilma?"

"Oh, the usual, Shirley. Was busy around lunch but then thinned out. I'll be glad to get home and rest my feet."

Shirley nodded and prepared her order pad, apron, and other tools of her trade.

"Oh!" Wilma added, "I made an extra ten bucks today." She continued when Shirley turned an expression of interest her way. "Some guy hit on me with the corniest line yet. He said he was a psychic. He gave me ten dollars and told me he could tell me which pocket I put it in."

"Yes," Shirley asked. "Did he get it right?"

"Doesn't matter," Wilma replied grinning. "He forgot that I deal with money all day long. I put a ten-dollar bill in all my pockets. Whatever he guessed, I showed him the bill from a different pocket."

The Fire

Eldon and Roberta Dawson were a quiet couple. They were getting up in age but had decided they wanted to adopt a child. After contracting with the BabyLove adoption agency, they found that twin toddlers was the only choice available. They were surprised and apprehensive because they expected a single child, but after a quick conversation, they agreed that twins would be perfect.

The twins were born into a poor marriage. Their parents, like many young couples, thought that by having a baby, their marriage problems would be solved. However, the birth of the twins made the situation worse for them. The infants' needs—potty-training, diaper-changing, and midnight feedings—added strain on top of the strains already in their relationship. After three years, they realized that and ended their marriage. The young couple put their babies up for adoption.

The twins were four-years old when Eldon and

Roberta requested adoption. Being older children and
twins, the BabyLove agency found it harder and harder to
dispatch them out to desiring and qualified parents: most
adopting parents wanted a single infant. When Eldon and
Roberta requested adopting the twins, the BabyLove
agency quickly closed the deal.

The adoption agency took into account that Eldon
was a retired schoolteacher and Roberta had spent several
years assisting in a day care center at one time in her life.
Because the babies were past the age of infancy and those
kinds of demands, the adoption agency decided that Eldon
and Roberta were a suitable fit. The BabyLove agency
signed over the toddlers, Clyde and Cleo, to their new
parents. Although the twins were too young to remember
their original parents when they were given up, they did
remember the drab and dreary life of the foster care
system that came after.

Roberta and Eldon were wonderful parents. They
brought love into the lives of Clyde and Cleo. The older
couple met all their physical needs, cared for them, gave
them attention and a life that contrasted sharply with their
previous life. Instead of being slapped on the wrist when
Cleo took an unpermitted cookie, Eldon offered her
another one. Instead of going to bed hungry if they
misbehaved, Clyde and Cleo never went to bed without
dinner, a warm bath, and a wonderful story read to them
each night.

Clyde and Cleo both remembered the weekly visits in

the summer to the ice cream store. Eldon would make a big deal out of it, pretend that it was a secret that "Mom" didn't need to know about, and experiment with the different flavors in different kinds of ice cream cones. The three of them would walk along the sidewalk licking the ice cream to keep it from melting onto their hands.

Roberta and Eldon taught the twins that life had consequences too. If the rules were broken, which didn't happen often, Clyde and Cleo knew exactly what to expect, and came to rely on that consistency. Sometimes they wanted to break a rule despite the consequences. When they decided to deliberately break a rule, they took the consequences as a matter of fact. Roberta and Eldon took that active decision of rule-breaking as a demonstration of maturing, and were happy about it.

Roberta and Eldon encouraged the children to think for themselves, to try different things, to be proactive about adventures. One day at the beach, the twins watched how other children sometimes would be knocked down by the waves. Some children ran crying back to their mothers but when that happened to Clyde and Cleo, they would laugh and run back into the waves, glad for the thrill.

Life with Roberta and Eldon Dawson was the best time of the twins' lives up to that point. Clyde and Cleo were happy until all that changed during their sixth year, when the twins were ten years old.

One of the rules imposed on Clyde and Cleo was not

to play with matches. One day, Cleo happened on a small butane lighter—a micro torch—and snuck off to another room to see what it was about. She sat on the couch near a window and pushed down on the switch. She was rewarded with a sharp blue flame and the steady hiss of gas.

Clyde followed her into the room, as he often followed her wherever she went, just as she frequently followed him. "You can't play with fire," he said, but was intrigued by the short blue flame that came from such a small pencil-shaped rod.

"Mom and Dad said not to play with matches," came her reply. "This isn't a match."

"It's still fire," Clyde persisted. "Same thing. Here, let me have it." He reached for it but Cleo pulled it away.

The butane lighter had a built-in safety switch so that if it was dropped, it immediately turned off so the flame would go out. However, when Clyde reached for the lighter, Cleo held on to it tighter as she swung it away. She didn't notice that it ignited the drapes near her.

As she and Clyde wrestled for the torch, it swung again across the drapes and lit them in another spot. Now the flames were impossible to miss. Cleo gasped, dropped the torch, and fled the room. Clyde saw the torch lying on the rug. Although the flame was out, the barrel was still hot and the rug began to smolder. He picked up the torch just as Eldon entered the room.

"What's all the ruckus about?" he started. Then he saw

the flames, which had moved up the drapes. Shreds of flaming material fell to the couch, burning its upholstery. In seconds, the flames were licking the ceiling and Eldon knew they were out of his control. He stared in an unbelieving moment at Clyde holding the butane torch. He grabbed Clyde by the arm and dragged him from the room. He then ran off to call the fire department.

The fire department arrived and quickly extinguished the fire. Several rooms were destroyed, some by fire and some by water damage, but the house was mostly intact. The firefighters gathered up their hoses and tools.

Clyde, Cleo, and Eldon stood on the front lawn, staring incredulously, and not believing that the fire could spread so rapidly. They strained their eyes looking nervously for Roberta to emerge from the house, but no Roberta.

Several firemen discussed something serious near one of the fire trucks. The EMTs gurneyed a body covered in a sheet from the fire-scorched house into their ambulance. Eldon ran toward the ambulance but one of the firemen stopped him.

"I'm sorry for your loss," he said. "She was in the attic and died of smoke inhalation." The fireman escorted him to the ambulance and nodded to the EMT. Eldon climbed in and the ambulance drove away. Clyde and Cleo stared desolately at the ambulance and then at the house. It was the last time that Clyde ever saw Eldon.

One may wonder what the twins were thinking as the ambulance drove away. Were they thinking about how they were going to cope with grief? Or with the loss of their adopted mother? Were they wondering how such a drastic change of affairs in their life could have happened? Did they wonder what Eldon would do to them since he knew they had started the fire? Would he send back to the foster care system?

Mostly, being ten years old and never in such a situation before, they were in shock. They merely stood and stared. Slowly they realized that Eldon had left them behind when the ambulance sirened off to the hospital.

The police talked with the twins for awhile, then Mrs. Malbury of foster care services showed up and talked with the twins for awhile longer. With the adopted mother dead, their foster status was in question. She scheduled two nights at a foster home for them until "their foster status could be sorted."

The hospital was decent enough to allow Eldon to sit with Roberta in a comfortable room all night until, as a staff member put it, "she simply must be transported downstairs." The staff were all sorry for his loss.

Mrs. Malbury approached Eldon at the hospital. She bluntly asked what Eldon wanted to do with the twins. Eldon, recalling Clyde with a butane torch in his hand while the wall crackled in flames, said, "I don't ever want to see Clyde again."

Mrs. Malbury assumed that Eldon meant he wanted

to un-adopt Clyde. From a simple statement spawned from grief, and the assumption by an agent from a callous bureaucracy, Clyde was returned into the system, but not the one to which he was familiar.

He was a prime suspect in the arson, so was sent to a juvenile detention center. It was the first time he was separated from Cleo and the first time he was in such a harsh environment. In foster homes, at least the parents *pretended* to care for their charges. In juvie, he had to be careful not to become a target of older inmates. Clyde's sense of injustice grew and deepened the longer he was in that system—until it turned to hate.

Eldon returned home and Cleo stayed with him. In his grief, Eldon neglected himself. He neglected her. She was in shock as much of losing Clyde as she was of losing Roberta. Although she was old enough to get herself dressed and eat boxed cereal for her meals and get ready for bed, she didn't go to school. She talked only when spoken to.

Eldon didn't talk to her at all—he was submerged in a sea of loss. Cleo roamed the house for weeks, a phantom of herself that haunted her old life.

For the first time in her life—no Eldon, no Roberta, no Clyde—she was set upon by uncontrolled guilt and loneliness, partially for starting the fire that killed her Mom, and partially for Clyde being sent to juvie. She had let him take the blame. Slowly, she realized that if Clyde had not fought with her, the fire would not have started, so she concluded: Clyde *was* responsible for Mom's death.

Three weeks later, Eldon committed suicide and Cleo was returned to the foster care system. This time she was sent separately from her twin brother instead of with him as was done numerous times before. She blamed Clyde for the fire, for killing Roberta, and for being returned back into the system. She blamed Clyde for the loss of the happiest days of her life, now all gone.

Clyde and Cleo were released into society after their eighteenth birthday. The juvie and foster care systems were in the same county, so they were given jobs and temporary places to stay in two nearby cities: Cleo was placed in the small town of Emberlin, and Clyde into Burgerville about 30 miles away. The system then ignored them and let them go their way—they were adults now and of no concern to the system.

Time in the emotionless system had shattered their self-esteem and ambition. Although they lived near each other, they didn't know that. They never saw each other and never tried to reach out to find each other. They accepted everything in the lackluster way they had, a drab indifference that had developed into a habit of mind, into an attitude.

Cleo took a job as a server at the local cafe. She was pretty and received extra tips at first, which she received without comment, until the regulars got to know her better. Her lack of interaction, and sometimes snarky responses, with someone who expected a thank you or even a smile, resulted in her barely getting tipped at all by her regulars. That only confirmed to Cleo that the world was an unlikable place and didn't deserve her attention. It became an established fact in her mind.

Soon she began to associate with the more unsavory people in her community. She learned about drugs and larceny and how to look out for herself, regardless of the consequences to other people. Being pretty, she was instructed on how to set up victims for her associates.

Her closest associate, if "close" applied to anyone in Cleo's life, was a sleazy street rat named Worm. He hung out in the dives and back-alley gambling halls, mugging people when he needed money. He had no regular job and was a snort away from drug addiction.

His daily "job" was casing residences and breaking & entering to steal their electronics. He was well-known to the local stolen-goods fences and knew some of the policemen by their first names. Most of the local policemen knew Worm's real name and rap sheet.

Clyde's situation was similar to Cleo's. The juvie system gave Clyde to Bill, a mechanic who brought him on board at his run-down service station. At first Bill was happy for the extra help, and looked forward to being a mentor to this orphan. Bill taught Clyde about automobile mechanics and Clyde was a fast learner.

However, Clyde liked being alone, and repairing cars and trucks allowed that to happen. He was resigned to the endless dullness of his life. He had little interaction with customers, and was often left on his own. He rarely said anything, even when asked.

After a time, Bill gave in to the idea that Clyde was not going to become a work partner. Bill realized that Clyde wanted to be alone, and it was too hard to get Clyde to open up to him. Soon Bill ignored him in the shop as long as Clyde did his job.

Bill was generally honest but he needed to make money. One day Bill needed a special part for a particular brand of car and none of his local suppliers had one. He told Clyde to see if Larry's Scrap Yard in Emberlin had one.

Larry's Scrap Yard was a junkyard of broken cars from which Larry would sell parts. Bill knew that Larry was on the sleazy side but a needed part was a needed part, and the repair fee was money in his pocket. If Larry was doing anything illegal, Bill didn't know about it. He didn't want to know about it. Don't ask, don't tell.

Clyde drove to Emberlin and walked into the sales room, if that was what it could be called. The room stank of cigarette smoke and grease and body odor. Old partially rusted parts hung on the wall like trophies, with small, slightly crumpled paper signs that said, "On Sale Today".

Larry was an overweight and short man, with a sweaty face that only his mother might trust. He stood behind the sales counter in a dirty leather apron and smoked a cigar out of the side of his mouth.

After Clyde told Larry what he wanted, Larry shook his head. "Don't know where one of those might be. You can check the yard," and tilted his head back over his shoulder, indicating the general direction of his vehicular graveyard.

"If you find it, bring it to the front here," Larry continued. "If it's still attached, you'll have to remove it yourself. I have no one here today to do that for you."

It seemed unlikely that Larry ever had anyone to remove parts from cars. Now Clyde knew why Bill told him to take his tools along.

"Bring it here to the sales counter and pay for it," Larry told him. "I can't leave the sales room."

Clyde looked around the small room. Calling the cracked and bumpy counter with a cash register and several burn marks on it a sales counter was an extravagance; calling this smelly dingy room a sales room was verbally perfuming the pig.

Clyde left the "sales room" and wandered through the acres of car and truck corpses, hunting for the brand of car he needed. Occasionally, he would find it, but the framistan he needed was already gone. He spent hours, getting more frustrated with every vain attempt. As he walked past car after car, he realized that he was like these discarded vehicles. Despite being eighteen years old, he felt used up, a nothing in a field of discarded nothings. His frustration at not being able to find one single part in the vast expanse of parts made him feel useless and put him in a bad mood.

Eventually, he found the kind of car he needed that had a working framistan. He got his tools from his car and removed the part, which he took back with him to Larry's, along with a set of banged knuckles and a stubbed shin. His bad mood had worsened.

Worm drove to Larry's Scrap Yard on his greasy motorcycle with Cleo on the back. She and Worm had moved up a rung in the larceny ladder. They hoped to sell parts to Larry from a stolen car for a good payout.

Cleo was already planning on how she was going to spend her money from this latest heist. She wore her best come-hither ensemble: a pleated purple miniskirt, a tight tank top, and her "cool" boots in the hopes that if Larry saw her, it would enhance the deal. She had even practiced smiling.

"I don't know why we had to come on this thing," she said, nodding to the motorcycle. "Why didn't we take the car? Larry could look at it and perhaps swing a better deal."

"Well, honey cheeks," Worm replied, all smarmy like he was. "There may be a report out for it, and I don't want to be caught with it—and neither do you. Besides, Turk hasn't had time to strip it yet."

Cleo nodded, thinking that made sense.

"Let's just see what Larry wants to give for the parts,"

Worm said as he walked into the storefront.

The deal was short, very short because there was no deal. Although Larry and Worm knew each other well enough, Larry complained about amateurs selling parts that could be traced back to him. Also, there were too many hot cars all over town right now, and Larry was already taking too many risks from the pros. No deal.

Worm and Cleo didn't know what to do. Cleo was expecting a slam-dunk deal. Worm had said so. Worm did the only thing he knew to do when he was blocked: just keep trying, getting oilier and sleazier at each attempt. Worm continued to plead for Larry to take a chance on him, promising that he, Worm, was very skillful and the parts could not be traced back to him.

After a few minutes, Cleo in her disappointment huffed out "Whatever!" and stalked from the shop. She walked along the parking lot gravel and lit a cigarette. That's when Clyde turned the corner and stopped short in front of Cleo.

They stared at each other, stunned. Through the distance of time, both had changed a lot as they grew older, but not enough for them not to recognize each other. Neither spoke for a moment.

"What are *you* doing here?" Cleo started, almost angrily.

Clyde didn't know what to say. He held up the ten-pound framistan in his hand, as if that explained everything.

Worm left Larry's sales room in bitter disappointment and anger. Then he saw Cleo arguing with some guy. He stopped dead. *Who's this guy,* Worm asked himself. *Is this one of her old boyfriends trying to get her back?* Worm would not stand for someone making moves on his girlfriend, or trying to take over his territory. *No, not today!*

Without hearing any of the conversation, Worm stalked forward and shoved himself in-between them. "No means no, Mac! Piss off!" He shoved Clyde on the shoulder.

Clyde, surprised, rocked back a step, which only encouraged Worm to try again. He pushed Clyde back again. *No one is messing with me today!* Worm thought.

Clyde had seem Worm's kind before. There were three kinds of people in juvie. The first kind was quiet and was the shot-caller for a group of mean kids. This kind didn't need to shout and rage because they always had their gang behind them.

The second kind were the bullies who got their way most of the time by shouting and threatening and intimidating, acting tougher than they actually were; bullies that liked to throw their weight around, as long as someone didn't push back.

The third kind was quiet, usually alone, but could take care of themselves. They stood up to bullies most of the time, and tried not to get in the way of the first kind. Clyde was the third kind. He recognized Worm as the second kind, a bully who pushed around the meth-heads and other

98

street rats in his own circle of associates.

After that second push, Clyde dropped the tool box and smacked him in the face with his free hand. Worm waded in, fists flying. Worm was a decent street fighter and could get what he wanted most of the time, but in juvie, Clyde fought to survive. Every battle he had could be deadly. Now this stranger came on to him, an interloper in family matters, and tried to push him around. From his already bad mood, Clyde slipped into survival mode. He exploded into Worm.

He jabbed at Worm with his free left hand, then slammed Worm with the heavy framistan in his right. He swung it back and hit Worm again on the return swing. Worm went down, blood flowing from his temple. Clyde raised the heavy metal part to smash Worm again if Worm tried to rise.

"Stop!" Cleo screamed. "Now look what you've done! You're always causing trouble." With that, years of painful memories flooded back, memories that blamed Clyde for all her woes.

"Causing trouble?" Clyde replied in disbelief. "He started it. What trouble did I cause?"

"You were always trouble, even when we were growing up. I was happy back then, but you went and messed that up," she started.

"Messed what up? You're the one that caused all the trouble." With that, now Clyde had years of painful memories flood back, memories that blamed Cleo for all his woes. "You started the fire! And then you said nothing when they hauled me away to juvie. Why didn't you say something?"

Cleo said nothing.

"Mom and Dad were the happiest times of my life," Clyde responded, "and you went and ruined all that."

"I did?!" she shouted in surprise.

Worm groaned, still lying unconscious in the gravel parking lot.

"Look," Cleo mentally stopped the tirade she was about to start, a tirade made from years of pain, "We need to get him to a hospital."

"Well, take him to the hospital then." Clyde turned and walked away.

"I can't," Cleo argued. "We came on that stupid bike--" she pointed to the motorcycle parked in front of the junk yard office. "I can't get him to a hospital on that!"

Clyde was deadly angry at Cleo, and at this asshole with her who he didn't know or care about. He didn't want to get involved with anything Cleo. But then again, he didn't want someone to die, especially someone he had just knocked out in a fight.

"Okay." Clyde muttered. "I'll pull my car around."

Within a few minutes, Worm was in the backseat bleeding into an old shop rag Clyde kept in his car. Cleo was in the front seat on her phone trying to find the closest hospital.

"Go straight up Route 13. There's one in about 15

100

minutes."

He peeled from the parking lot without paying for the framistan.

Neither twin said a word for a few minutes, both sat fuming in the front seat. Then Cleo started. "Living with Mom and Dad was the happiest time of my life too."

Clyde said nothing.

"Then you went and started that fire that killed her," Cleo continued.

"The fire I started?" Clyde sputtered. "You started the fire, and when I tried to stop you, I got blamed for it. When you said nothing, I went to juvie. For eight years, you just let me rot."

"If you hadn't fought with me, the fire wouldn't have started."

Clyde continued as if he hadn't heard. "Then you lived with Dad and killed him within the month."

"Killed him?" Cleo couldn't believe what she was hearing. "He committed suicide," she shouted back.

"So the official report said! But what is that worth, especially with you there to do all the talking. I don't want anything to do with you. Stay out of my life!"

"I was only ten!" Cleo stared straight ahead, still furious, then resolved. "Okay, fine! Pull off and I'll deal with this myself. I'll call 911 and let them take him."

"Yeah, sure!" Clyde responded. "Once I'm gone, it'll be all my fault—again. And this time, I actually did hit him."

"Just pull off!" Cleo grabbed the steering wheel and pulled hard. The car veered sharply to the right. The tires screeched in protest before it went onto the berm.

Clyde jerked the wheel back again. The car slid onto the pavement and jumped across the road. Cleo pulled the wheel to the right again. The car fishtailed and slid sideways. Clyde hit the brakes hard.

They had been moving fast toward the Route 13 bridge that ran over the Jordan River about 200 feet below. When Clyde hit the brakes, it slid into the cement block that fixed the bridge to the land. The car, sliding sideways into it, flipped over and rolled under its momentum. It rolled once, twice, three times. The car continued over the embankment until it crashed into the rocky sides of the cliff below. The gas tank caught a spark and the entire car exploded, killing Clyde, Cleo, and Worm. They all died in the fire.

Thus died the twins who wallowed in the ashes of their grief and could not get past the consequences of one fiery event in their life. From their grief, they struck out in anger at the only one they knew. The fire, eight years earlier, had scorched their happiest times and incinerated their lives.

Pecos Bay

Every year in late August, the hydroplane races are held at Pecos Bay. I used to spend my time racing, but now, with the onset of my forties, I have retired and spend my time sponsoring up-and-coming racers and their hydroplanes.

Racing is a young person's game, but I still love the thrill of the race. I love the feel and vibration of the powerboat chittering over the water's surface, the bump and thump as it flashes over small swells, even the fierce spray of water in my face. By sponsoring a potential racer, I feel I am still a part of it. I can enjoy the thrill vicariously.

A week before the race, I traveled down to Pecos Bay to check out my latest powerboat. I met with Frank Alonzo, the pilot and owner of the *Water Skimmer*. He had won most of the races in his circuit and I thought he would make a suitable bet. I wanted to take a personal first-hand look.

Even before settling into my hotel room, I visited the

boathouse where the *Water Skimmer* was docked. The boathouse was a ramshackle affair, afflicted with years of wet weather and winds. Gaps between the discolored boards let in the afternoon sun. As I entered, I was immediately immersed in the familiar smells of gasoline and grease and salt water.

The *Water Skimmer* was up in dry dock, but it still looked sleek and professional, beautifully painted with wavy streaks of green and white. With the sun glinting off her sides, and the water only a couple feet below, I could imagine the feel of racing her. I could almost feel the cramp in my hands on the wheel as she slammed over the open water to the finish line. I smiled a little at the image.

Frank came over and introduced himself, wiping his hands on a rag. He was a typical racer: fairly handsome, athletic and with a no-nonsense personality. I noticed that about people who face death frequently. They are generally good-looking, direct, and have no time for trivialities. I sometimes wondered as to why. I guessed that in comparison with death-defying activities, all else is trivial.

With him was a woman in grease-covered overalls. She had so much grease on her face that I could barely make out what she looked like.

"This is my assistant, Rebecca," Frank introduced her.

Rebecca stuck out her hand, realized it was covered in grease, and pulled it back. She merely smiled and nodded. Her brilliant white teeth shone out from her sun-tanned skin and tousled brown hair. She looked me directly in the eyes. It was hard to tell how old she was. "Becky," she said in a low rumble of a voice.

Even though I sported my typical denim shirt and jeans, I felt over-dressed. I wanted to be one of the insiders, a racer in my own right, and not merely the "money". I wanted to reach out and shake her grease-covered hand to prove it to her and Frank both. But I didn't.

"We're doing some last minute touch ups," Frank said. "We ran time trials yesterday and think we can get an extra half to three-quarter second out of her."

"That much?" I asked.

"Shouldn't be too hard," Becky said matter-of-factly. "We only need a few parts."

Frank cut in. "Of course, you'll want to see what she can do. Inspect her, and so on." He sent a glancing smile at Rebecca. "We can talk parts and money later."

"And the books," I responded.

"Of course, the books," Frank nodded.

I settled into the little town of Pecos Bay, which unsurprisingly was on the beach of Pecos Bay, a sheltered saltwater inlet of the south Atlantic. Normally, hydroplane races could not be held in ocean swells, but on most days, quiet days, the water of the bay was like glass, as flat as a tabletop. Saltwater meant extra maintenance, but that is why the purses for saltwater hydroplane races were slightly larger than for lakes and flat rivers.

Over the next few days, I inspected the boat, the engine, checked the controls, and looked over the books. Frank had done well for himself. He had no money problems and the boat was in great shape. I thought I had a good bet with Frank and the *Water Skimmer.*

During this time, I saw Rebecca now and then. Each time she would look intently in my direction. It was a mysterious expression, as if she wanted to say something but didn't. Sometimes we were too far away from each other to say anything without shouting. Sometimes she would smile and look away, which only served to heighten the mystery.

On the evening before the race, I sauntered down to the boathouse to give the boat one last look-over. The downing sun slanted in through the slats in the walls and gave the *Water Skimmer* a particular appeal. She sat rocking slowly on the surface of the water.

A wooden plank walkway, as weather-beaten and worn as the boathouse, extended from the beach to the interior. An outer door on the bayside of the structure opened to give the powerboat access to the water. It was open now, and I could see a couple young boys, maybe six or eight years old, wrestling on the sand as young kids do. An older boy, perhaps ten years old, intervened and tried to stop the friendly play, but soon all three were laughing and rolling in the sand.

Beside a large crate was a thick woolen blanket spread across the walkway. I lay down to get a lower perspective and stared at the craft floating there, representing my fortune if it won. I noticed something on the side of the boat.

Before I could resolve what it was, Rebecca flopped

down beside me. With the crate on one side and the edge of the blanket on the other, we touched along one side of our bodies. I could feel her warmth.

"Hi," she smiled. "Beautiful, isn't she?" I turned and saw that Rebecca still wore her greasy coveralls, and still had smudges on her face. Her fingernails were dirty and her hands calloused.

"Yes, it is. Will she win tomorrow?"

Rebecca chuckled, deep and throaty. "Aren't you the one betting on it?"

"Yes, I am." I grinned back. "She's a fine boat." We both stared at it in silence for a few moments. I imagined the race tomorrow. I could hear the roar of engines and imagine the other boats trailing behind her frothy white wake as she sped toward the finish line. I imagined it skimming over the surface of the water, crossing the finish line first. We would all celebrate together.

I remembered the mark on the hull. "What is that mark?" I pointed to the rear side just in front of the rudder.

"Where?" She was suddenly concerned. "I don't see anything."

I pointed again. I threw my arm that lie between us so that could move closer. I moved my head near hers so that we could look down my arm for a better view. Again, I was aware of her body and touch, the smell of grease, and the smell of her. "Do you see?"

She turned to look at me. Her eyes were a scant few inches from mine. Being this close, I saw that her skin was sun-drenched and tanned, but it was smooth and without blemish. She may have been younger than I originally thought. At the time, this was all innocent. I didn't realize that she may have thought that my placing my arm over her body was a come-on.

"Do you see the mark?" I asked

She pushed me over onto my back and rolled on top of me, her body lithe, her face still as close. "A mark, eh?" She paused and smiled. "Perhaps we should go down to my trailer and watch the recordings of the time trials. See if we find a mark there."

I'm not use to women rolling on top of me. I was taken aback at first, but I could not help but smile under that gleaming grin of hers.

Before I could respond, the older boy from outside swam into the boathouse and pulled himself onto the walkway near us.

"Becky," he complained. "I can't get the twins home. They just ignore me. You gotta say something."

"Go away, Manny," she said, still looking down into my face from above.

"Well, I should be going anyway." I gently pushed her off me and stood up. She also stood, but her face was dark and glowering.

"You don't take me seriously, mister?"

I didn't know what to say. "We have a big day tomorrow. We should get ready for the race," I said awkwardly.

She huffed and left with fast stomping strides.

I spent dinner wondering what had happened and why Rebecca was mad. In circumspect, my actions might have seemed out of place, but then, she was coming on to me. Still wondering if I did something to offend her or she misunderstood and over-reacted, I wandered back to the beach. The moon was full and the calm water reflected the panorama of stars above.

I saw Frank moving steadily in my direction. As he got closer, I saw he was angry.

"What did you do to Becky?" he accused. "Did you mess with her?" He was fuming mad. He stood braced as if he was going to take a punch at me.

"What?" I hadn't figured out what had happened myself with Becky. "I didn't do anything."

"Manny says he saw the two of you making out on the blanket in the boathouse."

"Manny was mistaken," was my only reply.

"Don't lie to me. I don't want your money bad enough to put up with this!" Now he actually did take a swing at me, or tried.

I caught his fist and straight-armed him in the chest, moving a few steps and pushing him up against an old water tower. I stared directly into his eyes, still holding him against the tower. I spoke slowly, with emphasis. "Nothing happened. And nothing is *going* to happen!"

He relaxed a little, like he believed me.

I lowered his fist and took my hand from his chest. "I came here to win a race, and jealous husbands I don't

109

need."

"What?" he exploded. "I'm not her husband!"

"Well then, jealous boyfriends. Besides, her kid was there with us for part of the time. What could we do if we had wanted?"

"Her kid?" Frank was as confused as I had been an hour ago. "That was her brother! Becky is my daughter, and she's only 18!"

Some many trains of thought derailed in my head that I was speechless, so I said nothing. I stood on the beach with a dumb expression on my face. Frank shook his head. I thought he was going to apologize, or maybe he thought I should apologize, but he merely walked away. "See you tomorrow at the race," he muttered.

The next day, I wondered what would happen when Frank and Rebecca and I met again at the race. Frank's bay cruiser took me out into the bay for a better look at the race. I was surprised to find him a few minutes later standing beside me.

"Good morning!" He was cheerful and friendly, as if nothing had happened last night.

"Aren't you racing?" I worried that he may have been angry enough with me to drop from the race, perhaps from spite. That would not be typical racer behavior: it's hard to stop an avid racer from racing. Also, so much was on the line with the race, but I didn't know how deep his fatherly instincts were to protect his daughter. Perhaps he would risk money to spite me. I would lose a goodly amount if that was the case, and he knew it.

110

"Not today." I heard the rumble of the powerboat turning over slowly as the *Water Skimmer* came up along side the cruiser.

"Becky is the pilot. She's a better racer than me anyway. It is because of her that we have won this year. I'm getting a little on the gray side of this sport." He paused and stared at the horizon. "She said she wanted to prove something." He looked at me from the corner of his eye. "I wonder what?"

The powerboat slid alongside us. For the first time I saw Rebecca not in greasy coveralls. She wore an aquamarine swimsuit that matched the paint of the hydroplane. Both had the racing number 22 across it, and she was all woman. She was not the mother I thought she was or the weathered mechanic, but an eager 18 year old pilot about to win my race.

She stared squarely into my face. "I'm going to win this race for you, Mister Perkins."

She said it with such conviction! She was hungry to win. I knew it was true. I didn't wonder about what she was trying to prove and I didn't care *why*. I didn't care whether she had a crush on me or wanted to impress her first sponsor or wanted to impress her father or because this was her first official race of the year. Either way, I looked forward to a long winning season.

Plots from Literary Estates

Chess Stories

I've always felt that the battle between the Light and Dark forces on a chessboard could be the skeleton for a story plot. Since I am inclined to fantasy adventure stories, for my first foray into this area, I concocted a plot with a medieval war theme. The first story is based on one of the shortest games known: a four-move game called Scholar's Mate, and thus the name of the story.

I was concerned about the ending: How could the light queen neutralize the dark king without killing him, since the king is never killed in a game of chess. I resolved it with a political answer. In case the reader would like to play the game in synchronization with the plot points of the story, I included the actual chess moves as part of the "chapter titles."

The second story, *Chess Opera*, uses the most famous chess game of all time. It is the game most taught in chess classes and used for examples of great play.

German nobleman, Karl II, Duke of Brunswick, and the French aristocrat, Comte Isouard de Vauvenargues, played as partners against the greatest player in the world at the time, Paul Morphy. The game was played at a French opera house in 1858. Morphy played while he watched the opera with the board behind him! He defeated them handily. (Morphy got bored winning games after four years and went back to his law profession.)

Writing these two stories taught me a new perspective between chess and writing. Chess is full of action. Pieces are lost constantly, which translates in a story to a carousel of characters dying. Consequently, it is hard to maintain an engaging protagonist or antagonist to propel the story forward; without that, the story is less relatable to the readers.

As a result, I wanted the reader to like the good guys and dislike the bad guys. That's why I chose a cold war setting in *Chess Opera*, where secret agents are constantly being killed by each other (at least in the movies), and giving their all for their country or ideology.

For chess aficionados, *Chess Opera* has a handful of Easter eggs—hidden references to the historic Chess Opera game, as well as other cultural icons, games, players, and locations. See if you can find some.

Scholar's Mate

Two Guards
(e4 ...e5)

Olaf adjusted his armor as he ran down the trail to his post at the River. He was cutting it close, the penalty of death looming over him if he was late. The trail opened into a much-used clearing with last night's embers still glowing in the fire pit. The water of the River weakly lapped against the shore.

The River was not particularly wide or deep—barely a challenge to someone who wanted to cross it—but it was an impenetrable barrier, like all political boundaries whose violation was an act of war.

He saw Stevens standing in the sunlight near the fire pit, all packed up and waiting. "I was thinking you weren't going to make it," Stevens scowled. Stevens was a member of the Light Guard who was posted to the night shift.

Out of breath, Olaf merely shook his head. Without another word, Stevens hoisted his pack and trudged into

115

the forest back to the castle, the weariness of standing guard all night showing in his gait. No sooner had Olaf seated himself on the log that served as a watching post than another guard approached on the opposite side of the bank—a member of the Dark Guard. *Who was it this time?* Olaf thought. *Blankenship? No. Brugels.*

The guard glared across at Olaf. To make a point, Brugels walked to the water's edge and pulled his sword. He began to sharpen it, or pretend to. All Dark Guards kept their weapons and armor in top shape, just as the Light Guards did, and both of the fighters knew it. Brugels stared across at Olaf and smiled menacingly.

Olaf got the message. He knew Brugels. This was simply Brugels sending a message, a hint that he was waiting for the war to start, and then Brugels would be there for him.

Olaf was not concerned. He had fought his share of Dark Guards. Although Brugels was meaner than most, Olaf bet his skill against Brugel's any day. Olaf responded to Brugel's taunt with an exaggerated yawn and looked around the bank unconcerned.

Brugels grunted, sheathed his sword, and sat on the log near his fire pit. The Dark Guard stared at the Light Guard and the Light Guard stared back. Two fighters in identical guard posts across from each other at the same point on the River boundary.

Bishop's Gambit (Bc4 …Nc6)

Bishop Mercer had prepared all he could for this trip. Now it was time to step out and confront the enemy, an enemy that Mercer must treat as a friend. He adjusted his mace and cowl and walked down the lane toward his appointed position. On the way, he passed the trail that led to Olaf's guard post.

It won't hurt to check on status, Mercer thought. Anything to delay what might be coming. Mercer had a role to play, a key tactic in the king's strategy, but it could get him killed.

"Morning, guard," Mercer stepped from the forest trail and greeted Olaf.

Olaf, from habit, jumped to attention until he saw it was merely the bishop. He relaxed slightly. "Morning, sire."

"All calm on the southern front?"

Olaf glanced across the River at Brugels. Brugels stood. He could tell that something was happening when a high member of the king's court checked lowly guard posts.

"All is well," Olaf replied. "There's hardly any resistance today. Nothing to worry about." He spoke loudly so Brugels would be sure to hear him.

Mercer watched Brugels, no emotion showing on either man's face.

"Very well. Keep up the good work." It was a lame thing to say, but Mercer could think of nothing better at the moment. He glanced once more at Brugels and returned to the lane along the forest trail.

Two hours later, Bishop Mercer stood on the podium in the market square, which contained many more citizens of the Dark Kingdom than Mercer preferred. Usually he was cheered by having a large audience, but this time... The Light Bishop prepared to address them.

The members of the enemy court stood behind a wall of guards of the Dark Kingdom as if the bishop was a threat to them. The king scowled slightly. The queen wore her expression like a blank mask. Other court officials looked bored.

Mercer tried to minimize the danger he felt. The Dark Guards were only doing their duty, Mercer rationalized, but it didn't matter. This façade of a speech was not his prime reason for being here. He coughed slightly and began. He talked of peace and God and the evils of war. He was a blameless emissary of peace. Who could object?

Shortly after Mercer started his speech, a Dark Knight pushed through the wall of guards. He stood in front of the guards with arms crossed. At the slightest nod from the king or queen, a short stride and hop to the podium would put the knight's sword edge to the enemy bishop.

Mercer recognized this knight: Driscoll, a huge and fierce warrior. Driscoll wasn't buying a word of what Mercer was selling. Mercer kept a wary eye on him as he continued speaking, not breaking his verbal momentum. Word after word flowed from Mercer in the manner of any practiced speaker. He controlled his habit to break into sermonizing. He tried to make his speech a reasoned exemplar of objectivity and fairness.

Mercer wondered if Driscoll was onto him; or at the least, if the knight's presence would make his next move a bit harder.

A page stepped onto the podium and passed a note to Mercer, who paused and read it. Driscoll slid his hand to his sword. He stepped onto the podium and snatched the note from Mercer's hand. It was a simple scrawl, the content of which was not worth interrupting the speech. It told Mercer that his horse was installed at Kimble's Stable and was well fed and groomed. Driscoll huffed and returned to his place in front of the wall of Dark Guards.

Fortunately, Mercer had prearranged the message to be code for what was coming next. He hoped that it looked exactly like it seemed without revealing what it actually was. The note had come not from Kimble, but from Glasson, Mercer's inside informant.

Driscoll seemed satisfied that noting was afoot so Mercer relaxed slightly. However, if the note was discovered to have come from one of the Dark King's personal guards, it would not go well with Mercer—or the guard. It would mean death by torture for poor Glasson.

Light Bishop Mercer had spent months working Glasson, trying to achieve a friendship, putting pressure on him, and directing him to the needs of the Light King, which Mercer described as the moral high ground. Slowly, Glasson began to turn toward Mercer's goals.

Mercer had turned Glasson on the idea that Glasson's

job, protecting his Dark King—ostensibly a good man who made bad decisions—was an evil thing to do. Protecting an evil meant that Glasson was evil. How could God love an evil person? It was up to Glasson to help Mercer save lives.

Although all guards were selected by the king and queen to be the most loyal, slowly Glasson agreed with the bishop, and turned to "the light side". Glasson tried his best to follow "God's will". Now he agreed to follow God's will as interpreted by Bishop Mercer.

Mercer ended his speech on the podium and asked his audience to share his mission of peace. The king and queen turned away, which indicated to the court that they should also turn away. The guards kept their stoic expressions. Mercer knew he would not have another chance to address this court again.

Mercer left the podium and kept his hand in his pocket over the note until he was out of sight of the crowd. Then he glanced down at the small piece of paper. The note, quickly written, told Mercer when the king would be alone tomorrow: the time to strike!

Queen's Gambit (Qh5 ...Nf6)

Queen Agatha, the Light Queen, announced her tour. She would travel to lands along the border, spreading good tidings, encouraging the troops, and trying to convince the Dark Army that she was on a mission of peace. She would end at Rook's Landing, or so she said. Having the Light

Queen out and about was a dangerous move in itself, but Rook's Landing was especially dangerous because she would be within reach of the Dark Army's forces. She was a high-value target. Although the Light King felt uncomfortable with this action, he agreed that it would be worth the risk if all went well.

Agatha first moved her entourage to Lady's Leap, closer to the Dark castle but well within the Light border and safely among her forces. With great show, she set her tents and elaborately prepared for her outgoing journey. To all watchers, she was readying her tour closer into enemy territory at Rook's Landing.

Agatha knew that an ambush probably awaited her; but if all went well, the Dark forces would be focused on the wrong place at the wrong time.

As expected, the Dark King's guard moved his forces nearer to Rook's Landing. More Dark forces prepared to support those. They lay in wait in the forest, waiting for the Light Queen to approach her published destination.

The Time to Strike (Qxf7#)

The time had come. Agatha, bundled in peasant clothes, crawled into the merchant's wagon and settled herself for the dangerous journey. She waited in darkness in the back of the wagon as it left the safety of her home realm. The wagon bounced and jostled her about, violence that she had not experienced much in her royal life.

Agatha was stalwart though and withstood the

onslaught of the road with little thought for herself. She thought instead of what she must do. As queen, she was executing an operation that could stop a war if it was successful, or make her dead if it was not.

The wagon reached the border and two Dark Guards zealously questioned the merchant and his wife. They opened the back to reveal the peasant girl, trembling in the back. Agatha thought her trembling act was insightful and well done, her bowing and groveling an award-winning performance. The guards smirked at her and closed the wagon. They waved the merchant through, on to the Dark castle.

Agatha left the wagon before the castle was in view. If Glasson had done his job, all would go well. She trudged down a forest trail in the dusk toward the back of the castle. It felt odd relying on the actions of an enemy.

Yes, Glasson had come through. The postern gate to the castle was unlocked as she had hoped. She eased herself inside and was met by a Dark Guard.

"Halt! Who goes there!" the guard barked.

She stood paralyzed. *Glasson had said nothing about a guard, but then, what did she expect? Her castle's captain always posted one or two guards at the back door to their fortifications too.* Before she could reply, or even think of a reply, Glasson called out from the courtyard path.

"Naughty girl, Melissa!" Glasson scolded her. "You know better than to stay out after gate-fall. The queen will be angry if she finds out." Glasson turned to the other guard. "Brinder, I'll take her from here." He lowered his voice, "She owes me a favor now." He winked.

Brinder smiled knowingly and stepped aside.

"I'm sorry, sire," Agatha said, in her best serving girl voice as she and Glasson walked closer to the castle. "I—I didn't know how late it was."

"Don't talk about that. I know that you go out there almost every evening. And I know who you meet. I don't know what you see in that mason boy anyway. If someone finds out he was also out after gate-fall, he will have his own troubles." Their voices faded with distance as they left Brinder and their falsified story at the postern gate.

Quietly Glasson led Agatha into the castle interior. Glasson picked a tray of food from a shelf that he had put aside for this occasion. He gave it to Agatha and led the queen along the castle passageways, pretending to scold her whenever someone approached.

At one point when they were alone, the queen pulled two leather coin pouches from somewhere deep inside her coarse coverings and handed them to him.

"You have done God's work tonight," she said.

Glasson stashed the pouches in his tunic.

"Get to Bishop Mercer after I'm inside," Agatha whispered.

They proceeded down the corridors until they stopped outside a heavily barred door. Two brawny guards stood outside.

"His lordship wanted something sweet tonight," Glasson said to one of the guards.

Agatha curtsied, bowed her head, and lifted the tray of

foodstuffs out before her.

"Yeah, I wouldn't be surprised," said one guard. "Are you talking about the food or the wench?" Both guards laughed at the joke.

Glasson went along with a mild chuckle. "As if I haven't heard that one before."

The guard on the right opened the door to the Dark King's chamber. Agatha stepped inside. She stood still, allowing her eyes to adjust to the dimness.

The king heard the door close and entered from an adjacent room. "What?" He stopped in surprise. He was half-undressed, his outer linen already removed.

"Are you alone, milord?" Agatha half-smiled. She moved slowly closer to the king.

The king glanced around the room and back at the door to the adjacent room. "Ah…yes," puzzlement across his face.

Agatha put the tray on the closest bureau and began removing her peasant clothes, one item at a time, as she approached the king.

"Remove your clothes." Her voice was sharper now but still low. It was not a request. She pulled a dagger from somewhere in her outer garments and raised it above her head.

"Well," the king smiled. "This could be very interesting." He pulled off his undergarments and threw them on the floor. He walked toward her with no concern for her dagger. She held it like a scullery maid, high in one hand as if this was the first time she had wielded a dagger.

She appeared to the king to be a mere maid who might be trying to blackmail him for her betterment. "This could be very interesting indeed!" he said.

As he closed on her, ready to take the dagger from her, he stopped short in surprise. He recognized her as the Light Queen in disguise.

"Yes, this will be very interesting." Agatha's voice was no longer timid but menacing, with a smirk on her face as she pushed a second dagger up from a hidden lower position. The dagger that she had shown first was only a ruse, a feint. As she had expected, the arrogant king had focused on the dagger she held in view, and he didn't notice the one in her other hand.

Too late the king realized she had switched to a classic two-dagger offense and a trained fighter's stance. *Of course the queen is trained in fighting,* he thought too late.

She removed the remainder of her peasant garb and revealed her royal garments that had been hidden beneath them. Now stood Queen Agatha in all her regalia, with a naked King Lionel in front of her. She ripped the top of her tunic to expose her bare shoulder. She tore the bottom of her dress, revealing one long leg.

"I don't know what you're doing, but one call to my guards and you are done!" the king warned.

Agatha began screaming at the top of her lungs. Lionel's eyes blinked in surprise.

Immediately the two guards outside the door burst in with swords raised. The king stared at the scene playing out before him, his mouth open.

125

The king still did not understand the situation. "What are you doing here?" he demanded of Agatha.

"We heard a scream," one guard said.

"Not you, fool!" The king shouted back.

A Dark Knight and Dark Bishop entered the room with two more guards. They stopped abruptly when they saw the naked king and enemy queen. Queen Agatha fell back on the bed as if in a swoon, secreting her daggers beneath the goose-down mattress.

"He tried to kill me after first having his way with me," she cried aloud.

"Sire!" This from the bishop in shocked amazement.

"What? That's preposterous!" the king exclaimed. The others were silent, not sure of what to believe; or perhaps not sure of contradicting their king.

The Dark Queen pushed her way into the room. "Lionel, what in the kingdom—" she started, then broke off with a gasp. "Lionel! What are you doing?"

"It's a trick," Lionel tried to explain. "She came in here dressed as a peasant and ripped her clothes and… and…she had two daggers…" Even he knew how silly he sounded. "Miriam, you must believe me."

"She ripped her own clothes?" the queen retorted dubiously. "And I suppose she took off your clothes too."

"Oh, no, she told me to take them off."

The guards tried to hide a chuckle beneath stern faces but couldn't. The Dark Queen shooed them all from the room. Only now did the king see that Light Bishop Mercer had come in behind Queen Miriam.

"What is *he* doing here?" Lionel demanded.

"It's a good thing he is. Bishop Mercer brought proof of the cad that you are. Ambushing an enemy is one thing, but capturing the enemy under a flag of truce for your personal wishes is low even for you!" She threw a rolled parchment at Lionel's naked form. "Cover yourself with this!"

Agatha slowly retreated behind Mercer.

"What is…." The king read from the note. *After you capture the queen at Rook's Landing, be sure to bring her to me first. No need to mention this to Queen Miriam. (signed) King Lionel.* He looked up desperately at Miriam. "I didn't write this!"

"No?" Miriam glared at him accusingly. "Is that your seal on it?"

"Yes, but…"

"Did you plan an ambush?"

"Yes, but…"

"Did you plan on taking the Light Queen for yourself, in secret?"

"Yes…no. Not like that."

"Glasson!" Queen Miriam shouted. "Glasson!"

Glasson of the king's personal guard, stepped into the room. "Glasson, place this…this… man," she said disdainfully, "in the dungeon. If he gives you any trouble, club him."

Glasson looked at the queen and then the king. He glanced furtively at Bishop Mercer, who gave the barest of nods.

Glasson called out, "Horace! Tarkinson!"

The two brawny guards entered again, stood at attention, and saluted Glasson. They knew this was a delicate situation and they were not going to let the least infraction of protocol get them in trouble. Both their king and queen were in a red-hot rage and they didn't want any of that heat to flow over onto them.

Mercer handed a nearby robe to the king.

Glasson turned to the king. "Sire?" He motioned to the doorway. "This will soon be sorted out."

Queen Miriam merely snorted. King Lionel stomped through the doorway into the hall. Miriam's back was ramrod straight as she slowly walked to Agatha.

"My lady Agatha, please let me make a formal apology to you. Please forgive this insult. Do not take this as an act of aggression to start a war, although you have every right. As you see, the perpetrator will be punished." She curtsied to Queen Agatha.

Queen Agatha made a show of straightening her clothes and smiled. "Thank you, Lady Miriam. I see now that it is personal and not an act of war against us. I suppose I should be flattered that the king went to so much trouble to acquire me. I will try to calm any revenge that King Henry may feel compelled to initiate, but…."

Agatha paused meaningfully. "Can we have a token to support that apology? Perhaps you can pull back your forces as a show of peace?"

Queen Miriam stiffened. She considered Agatha for a moment, then glanced at Bishop Mercer who had access to a public podium like all bishops. A scandal like this would paint both the king and queen in a very poor light and likely into a political corner.

She sighed. "Yes, we can do that. Anything to avert a war."

"Anything to avert a war," Agatha repeated. She bowed once to Miriam and left the room. Mercer followed close behind.

Queen Agatha and Bishop Mercer smiled slightly as they made their way back to their castle. Glasson smiled slightly at his post, thinking of all the good soldiers he had saved.

Plots from Literary Estates

Chess Opera

M & K Realty
(e4 ...e5)

Ken Paulson had mixed feelings as he returned from vacation. On the one hand, he enjoyed the two weeks he spent relaxing on the beach in Jamaica; on the other hand, he welcomed his return to fulfilling his small role in saving the world.

He pulled his new white 1955 Austin Healey speedster—a gift to himself during his vacation—into the parking lot in front of the single-story Paris cottage that sported a black and white sign out front: M & K Realty.

The realty office, known officially as Safe House Four, served as one of the agency's intelligence-gathering hubs—not for a realty agency, but for the government agency that supported the intelligence operations for which Ken worked. The small white cottage had been transformed by the government's security defenses to resemble a normal business office, but it was close to impenetrable.

Ken approached the door and noticed that it was locked. In his three years of working from this office, he had never seen the door locked. Of course, it could have happened, but not during a normal day. He and his partner Max left it unlocked when they were here to welcome potential clients looking to buy or sell houses.

In the front office, small bios of Ken and Max, and a few fictional realtors, hung on the walls, along with the expected membership plaque for the Better Business Bureau. On one desk sat a thick bound volume containing a collection of various listings that the operations office at headquarters kept up to date. There was even an award on the shelf for best realty group of last year; all for enhancing the cover of M & K Realty as a true realty agency.

During the evenings, other members of the agency inhabited the office. Sometimes, important persons were given temporary shelter when they passed through to other destinations. *Then* the doors could be locked, but the door should not have been locked at this hour.

Ken's training took over. He pulled his service weapon with one hand while he found his usually-unused key to unlock the front door. He turned off the alarms; one alarm in particular that alerted HQ to a break-in. He didn't want a SWAT team to come pouring down on him.

Where was his partner? Where was Max? He dared not call out. The rooms had not been cleared yet and someone could be waiting inside.

He moved from one room to another. Look left, then

right, weapon held vertically but ready for it to drop and shoot if the need suddenly arose. First one room, then another. Left, right, clear! Left, right, clear! Until Ken was sure that the front room, hallway, back office, and bathroom were empty of intruders.

No one in any of the rooms. He stopped in the back office of the cottage where he knew the communications equipment hid behind a vertically sliding panel. A wide glass bay window overlooked the ocean cove one block beyond. He checked the view for anything suspicious but saw only a few slow-moving boats as they moved out from their docks toward the ocean.

On the other side of the water, he could see the safe house of his opposite number, agent Blackbird. *Are they up to something they shouldn't?* he thought.

Ken knew that Blackbird's real name was Kevin Palintoff, but what did that matter? Ken's own code name, Polly, was better known to the intelligence community on both sides than his real name. He wasn't sure if even Max knew his real name. By the vagaries of some bureaucrat in the central operations codename office, Ken was Polly.

Polly rested his gun on the wooden counter below the bay window. He could see Blackbird drive into his building's parking lot on the other side of the cove and approach the entrance to his own operations hub in the Volksoper Tourist Center.

Did Blackbird seem preoccupied today? Polly couldn't be sure, but Blackbird usually sauntered into the building, sometimes whistling. Today, he paused several times to look around when he unlocked his car. He paused and stopped in mid-stride when checking his gun. He scanned the parking lot and vicinity furtively, checked his gun again, and quickly disappeared inside the "tourist center."

Is something going on over there, or am I jittery because the office was locked and Max isn't here? Polly wondered.

Still looking across the water, Polly saw a black sedan drive into the Volksoper tourist center parking lot. He picked up his binoculars from a nearby shelf and looked again. Yes! A woman was in the sedan with another man. They were not talking. Occasionally, she put her own pair of binoculars to her eyes in his direction.

Were they watching his safe house! he wondered. *Wait! No, they were watching the tourist center, and not him. Were they a support team for Blackbird? An attack team? Yes, something was happening today.*

Polly knew that they couldn't see through the back office bay window because it was refractive one-way glass. Still, it unnerved him. *What in the world are they up to?* he thought. *I doubt that you are birders trying to find the rare ruby-throated hummer or some such.*

Before Polly could follow his thoughts further, he heard a scratch, and a shifting from the front room, as of someone trying to move quietly. He picked his gun from the bay window counter, held it up, and put his back to the rear office wall. Someone was on the other side!

Enter Paladin (Nf3 ...d6)

Nathan Lang, a well-regarded field agent, pulled into the parking lot in front of M & K Realty. Before getting out of the car, he reviewed his orders in his head. *Orders were orders, but these seemed more urgent than usual: back up agent M. Currently, she was being briefed by Auntie, so he would wait for her to arrive.*

Nathan saw that the building's door was ajar. That should not be. He had not visited this office before but no safe house door was ever left ajar. *Locked or unlocked, maybe, but never ajar.* Agent M was not due to arrive yet and Polly was still on vacation until tomorrow. *Had the safe house been breached?*

Nathan quietly exited his car and shut the car door as quietly as he could. He pulled his gun and stealthily moved through the door of the realty office. He traversed the front room and found it clear, then he heard a noise in the rear office. He put his back to the rear office wall, gun up and ready; the other side of the same wall on which Polly was listening.

The Assassin Arrives (d4 ...g4)

Maxine Staunton, or Max, drove in silence as she returned to her post at the M & K Realty office. She enjoyed the curvy two-lane black-top road, her car's motor purring smoothly as she wound through the woods. She could see an ocean view through the trees to one side.

Max was stunned by what she had just been told in the briefing. Auntie—Max didn't know her real name—had only once before called her off-post for a briefing, so this must be important and urgent. Indeed it was: a credible threat against their Prime Minister, codename Shrike, had been intercepted and Max was to be the first agent to engage the enemy. Paladin himself had been assigned to her for backup.

For the last ten years, Max had gathered intelligence in Paris, a low-level kind of field ops. She enjoyed her time here. No real danger, more of a standby role.

Max knew she could be called up at any moment, but she thought those days were behind her. Her skills were rustier than she would have liked, and now she wouldn't have time to polish them to her old expertise. Although she spent time at the gym and in team practices to keep sharp, time erodes all skills. She would have liked time to acclimatize to the adrenalin rush of active fieldwork again, time she would not be given.

When Max arrived at Auntie's office, Auntie's assistant showed her right in. Auntie was the most senior ranked of the active agents and usually called the shots. She was in her late-thirties, blonde, tall, athletic and energetic. She was personable and warm but stayed distanced.

Although Max knew that the message was critically important, Auntie relayed it calmly as if over coffee with a friend. To an outsider, their conversation may have looked like one between two friends; they were both of roughly the same age. Max felt that she could easily become Auntie's friend, but over the last ten years and a series of occasional meetings, that never happened

Auntie was professional and precise. She laid out the operation carefully. Max asked many questions in the briefing, but few answers were known; or at least, were not being shared with her. "Above her pay grade" may be one reason for hiding information from her, but Auntie was too polite, at least for the moment, to play that card.

Max's orders: find out the answers to most of her (Max's) questions, the biggest one being, "Who is threatening the Prime Minster and how?" *The Why was obvious, as her country had been in cold war detente for years, so an op this big was not too surprising, but why now? And what would she find when she stepped into the other camp's territory, a step that could not be undone; a step that could drastically change world politics if it ever became public.*

Pulled from her reverie as she pulled up to the M & K Realty office, she turned off the engine to her car, a small compact model, suitable for a modest realtor in a modest realty office in the modest seaside town of Twin Rivers. It fit in well with the other typical cars already in the parking lot. Nothing to see here.

Max took a deep breath and checked her watch. She would soon meet Paladin and get further details. She started to get out of her car when she saw the office door was ajar. She knew she locked it when she left this morning. Now on instant alert, she scanned the parking lot looking for something—or someone—that shouldn't be there. There was a white Austin Healy sportster that she didn't know parked in the front row. *A potential client, or someone else?* she thought.

She reached into her purse and withdrew her nine millimeter Beretta. Small, light, and she knew how to use it with deadly accuracy, or at least she use to. She walked lightly to the door and slipped inside. She scanned the front room for intruders, then turned and silently closed the door and put the defense protocols in place to lockdown the safe house. *If someone wanted to leave quickly, that would slow them down.*

She moved down the hallway toward the back office and came across a stranger backed against the far wall. He was tall and brawny, with dark brown hair with the standard agency cut. He was not looking her way so she couldn't see his face.

"Freeze!" she shouted, snapping her Beretta toward him.

The man caught off guard, turned to fire, but recognized her from her dossier. He stopped. "M?"

Polly stepped from the other room, "Max?" Nathan jumped back in surprise as this other person stepped from behind him.

"Polly?" Max said.

The three stood there with guns drawn. Polly felt silly. "What are you doing here?" all three said simultaneously.

Max and Polly redirected their guns to the other man.

"What are you doing here," Max repeated.

"I'm Paladin. You're expecting me." He holstered his gun.

Polly and Max's guns never wavered. "I was expecting you outside. How did you get in?" Max demanded.

"The door was open. Wanted to check that the house wasn't breached," Paladin replied calmly.

"I returned from vacation a day early and saw that the door was locked. You never leave," Polly said to Max.

"Special order," she replied. "Something's up. Something big."

"Well, we're here now, so let's discuss the op," Paladin suggested.

Polly noticed that even with two guns directed at him, Paladin hadn't lost his cool. Polly and Max lowered their guns.

"Let's get you authorized first," Max said. She went to the back office and opened a sliding panel in the wall. It revealed the communication and verification equipment—fingerprint scanner, opcode transceiver, and the like.

Polly noted that Max opened the secret panel in front of a stranger. *She wouldn't have revealed the agency equipment in front of a stranger unless she was fairly certain Paladin was who he said he was.*

Max flipped a couple switches and was rewarded with the electronic hum of the equipment. "Code name and op name," she said dryly.

Paladin spoke without hesitation into the microphone.

139

Polly checked the voice print on the machine and declared, "You're clear."

Easy-Breezy (dxe5 …Bxf3)

Paladin took a place on the plush divan, Max sat in a nearby chair. Polly stood leaning against the hallway doorframe. "Fill us in," Polly asked casually.

Paladin started in a slow drawl that belied the import of his message. The other side had assigned a special contract assassin, known only by the codename Bishop. No one knew the real name. No pictures of him or her were available. None. Nothing to indicate even height, build, or race. He or she was a serious threat. Bishop charged high fees, but since Bishop was not known to fail, the fees were paid.

Paladin knew that Bishop planned to set up here in town, in Twin Rivers. For all Paladin knew, Bishop may already be in town somewhere. What was a highly paid assassin doing here at M & K Realty? Shrike was not here. It was too far for a sniper shot on Shrike for even the best snipers. Remote-controlled bomb? Possible, but unlikely, and too elaborate for the speed at which this op was setting up.

Max broke in, "Auntie says details of their plan may be in the Volksoper Tourist Center across the cove. It's possible Bishop is getting his instructions from there. It's my job to find out and report back."

The significance of that last statement was not lost on

Paladin. He stared at Max for a moment, nodded slightly.

"Okay," he said slowly. "Go in, find out what you can. It's not wet work, just simple intelligence gathering. In and out. Easy-breezy." Paladin said this as if she was about to walk down the street to catch a bus. "I'm here to help you stay out of trouble. Call out the code word 'Squash' and I'll come running, guns blazing." He smiled.

Noticing Max and Polly's expression, he quickly added, "But that's not likely.

Yeah, right.

A Visit to the Tourist Center (dxe5 ...Bxf3)

Max decided that with a black op in the making, enemy agents were probably watching their own safe house—the Volksoper Tourist Center—in case support was needed. Polly had alerted Paladin and Max to the couple watching from the Tourist Center's parking lot.

Max wanted to be careful. After she crossed the cove bridge over the waterway, she took the long way around, trying to avoid being seen.

For caution's sake, she entered by the side door. Of course, it was locked and wired to alarm for intruders, but that didn't matter. She only wanted to talk to their agent, to squeeze whatever information she could get from him.

After a few minutes at the lock, the door was open and the alarm stayed silent. She entered the spacious front room.

She remembered being here a couple of years ago. She

and Polly pretended to be tourists and wanted to scope out the building. *How safe was their enemy's safe house? What kind of threat did it contain?*

At the time, Polly and Max met an austere glowering woman with a sour attitude. While polite, she was not friendly. *She was probably put here meant to drive off tourists*, Max thought. Since then, she had been replaced with a man who they knew as Blackbird. Max had never met him.

The Center still contained a long counter facing the door, behind which someone could stand and discuss the attractions of the city with tourists. Behind the counter were racks of pamphlets describing local attractions. A row of wooden chairs sat against the wall facing the counter. The chairs accommodated, but were not so comfortable as to encourage visitors to stay too long.

No one in the front office. Max walked to the front door, pushed it open, let it close, and pretended she had just entered. As the door gave out the typical *bing! bong!* to alert the attendant, Max sat down in one of the chairs, one hand holding her gun out of sight beneath her purse.

Blackbird, the agent on duty, rushed from the back room through the doorway that opened beside the counter, his hand behind his back.

As I expected, he's armed, Max thought. *Does he meet all his tourists this way?*

Blackbird paused when he saw her sitting, then smiled and walked deliberately behind the counter.

Max tracked his motions in her mind. *He put his weapon*

under the counter. Out of sight but still within reach.

To disguise that action, Blackbird pulled some pamphlets from a rack on the counter and spread them on its flat surface.

Max had never met Blackbird before, but had seen his dossier pictures. Up close, he was a smaller man than Max had expected. He sported a thin pencil mustache and slicked-back hair. He reminded Max of the worst kind of used car salesman.

"Welcome to our fair city. How may I assist you, ma'am?" he hissed.

Max knew who he was and Blackbird knew who she was, and Max knew he knew. *Okay, fair enough. I'll keep the charade.* "I need some information," she responded.

Blackbird relaxed slightly, perhaps because he was not immediately being shot at. "Twin Rivers has a wide selection of stores for shopping. We have great museums, especially those for art and opera. If you like operas, we have the best in the land. Recently a new opera house opened, now showing Bellini's *Norma* to a packed house." He poked down a finger on each of the pamphlets as he pointed them out.

Max smiled slightly. "I need information about the Bishop."

Blackbird stiffened ever so slightly but kept his smile in place as his jaw tightened. "Well, if it's religion and cathedrals you want…" he almost drawled, "we have some of the finest ancient cathedrals in any city. There's St.

143

Karl's and St. Vauvenargues's cathedrals. Especially fine."

"No, not just any bishop. *The* Bishop. I need information about *the* Bishop, Kevin." Max added, revealing Blackbird's true name while keeping her hand on her Beretta. *If something was going to happen, it would happen now.*

Kevin was startled. He blinked. He paused, mouth half-open. He couldn't decide how to answer this question yet, but his eyes narrowed and he was tense again.

- * -

Sitting in the front room of M&K Realty, Paladin and Polly listened to the conversation between Max and Blackbird through a new innovative radio connection that one could wear in the ear. A bone microphone relayed verbal messages directly and clandestinely to the person on the other end of the transmission.

Get on with it, Paladin thought. *This namby-pamby polite conversation is getting us nowhere. Time is of the essence.*

Paladin was about to say that exact thing to Max when a bullet passed within inches of his ear. He heard the *Zorp!* of the compressed air as the bullet traveled toward him at supersonic speeds. He heard the crash of the bullet a microsecond afterward as it passed through the front window.

Paladin immediately identified the general direction of the shot. *It didn't come from across the cove, but across the street!*

144

The Philidor building!

He threw himself to the floor behind the divan. He knew he had been saved by the refraction window. The diffractive index of the glass was thick and formed so that what was seen was actually a couple inches to the left of where it was. A sniper, even knowing that, would have to guess in which direction the real target would be. The sniper guessed wrong.

Another shot passed through the divan and over his head into the back wall. A third bullet, ten inches lower, passed near Paladin's head even closer than the first one. The sniper's guesses were improving. Paladin looked around for a safer place.

Polly jumped to one side of the hallway and pulled his gun. He crouched behind its door jamb.

"Polly! Call Auntie!" Paladin shouted out. "Tell her we're under attack. We're pinned. Can't get to Max if she gets in trouble."

Polly flipped around and ran into the back office. He raised the panel concealing the short-wave set. He punched out the emergency code and spoke the message as fast as he could.

Max heard gunshots coming from the direction of her safe house. She heard the exchange between Paladin and Polly. She was on her own. *Should she return to her safe house or continue trying to get something from Blackbird?* Due to the urgency of her orders, she decided to stay.

Blackbird must have heard the shots too.

145

- * -

Auntie looked in the mirror and gave herself a quick self-appraisal. Her platinum blond hair hung down loosely over her form-fitting red dress that stopped several inches above her knees and long shapely legs. Her white clutch brought out the highlights in her hair and contrasted nicely with the red in her dress and lipstick. Although high heels would have been more in accord with the style, she never felt comfortable in high heels. It restricted movement and went against habits developed from years of training. Her experience won out. She prioritized survival over fashion.

Auntie gave an approving nod. She was ready to attend the gala tonight where she would confer with some members of the higher echelon of the Prime Minister's protection detail and her own Operations. It was a fancy affair, but served more as a summit meeting in light of the recent intel they had gathered, than for entertainment.

Her assistant Sofia rushed into the room. No knocking, no "excuse me, ma'am". That was the way Auntie trained her people for an emergency. Auntie knew she could have been naked in the bathtub and it wouldn't have mattered.

Sofia rushed over and passed a slip of blue paper— emergency message paper—into her hand and stood waiting. Auntie read it quickly.

"Tell Paladin I'm on my way. I'll be there in seven minutes. Ask him if he has the sniper's location. It's got to

146

be Bishop. Then tell the chief that I'll be late to tonight's gala."

Sofia nodded and rushed from the room.

- * -

Max heard gunshots coming from across the cove, in the direction of her safe house. *A high-powered rifle, Bishop's preferred weapon. Was Bishop here already and shooting at Polly and Paladin?* She strode to the nearest window to determine a location for the shooting. She moved her gun to a more suitable position in front of her.

Bam! The gunshot echoed inside her head. It was loud in the tourist center's front room. Then she felt the pain in her shoulder. *Weaselly punk-ass Kevin!* He had shot her when she turned to look out the window. Perhaps she was rustier than she thought. If she had not lost her edge, she wouldn't have taken her eyes off him, especially with an op in play.

So much for casual banter! She snapped reflexively back to him and pulled her trigger. It hit him high in his mid-section. He fell back into the hallway, then scooted backward out of sight.

Max was pissed! Fortunately, Blackbird had hit her left shoulder. Although she could shoot with either hand, she was right-handed and right-handed shooting gave her an advantage.

Max was wounded. She thought about calling out the

rescue code word 'Squash', but she knew Paladin was pinned down. Even though she was on her own, she thought she had the situation under control.

She leaned against the doorframe and called into the back room. "Kevin, you slug! I came here politely for some information and you have to act like that?"

Kevin groaned in pain. "You asked about the Bishop. No one's supposed to know about that," Kevin gasped out.

Max slowly advanced down the short hallway, and carefully entered the back room. Kevin was on the floor, one hand over his chest, which oozed red through his white shirt. "So what do you know about the Bishop? It seems he's already in play."

In answer, Kevin lifted his head and raised his gun to fire again. Max beat him to it. *Bam!* His head fell back on the floor with a thud that underscored the sound of her shot. Just then the front window exploded in crashing glass.

The man Polly had seen earlier in the black sedan ran forward, a gun in each hand. He crashed through the front window, firing continuously. He ran through the front room and into the back room. A fusillade of rounds smashed into the back office walls. Max was hit twice, then once more, before she fell.

The man closed on Max. He kicked away Max's gun from her hand. It skittered across the floor. He put his fingers alongside Kevin's neck. Max's eyes were closed but she was saying something, barely audible. He leaned in to hear.

"Squash. Squash," she whispered, barely conscious.

He moved to the equipment panel in the room and entered a code. The panel rose and revealed Blackbird's short wave set.

He hit a few buttons then spoke into the microphone. "Bull here. Yes, the Tourist Center. Blackbird's down. M is neutralized."

More was said on the other end of the line. "Tell the Duke and Countess their plan seems to be working," Bull said. A pause. "Okay, I'll be here." More listening. "Shouldn't be necessary but—Okay, copy. Send the cleaners."

He moved back to Max, put his gun to her head, and pulled the trigger.

– * –

Polly and Paladin could hear shots from across the cove. A few intermittent ones, then a volley of what seemed never-ending shots. Paladin could hear the same thing, but louder, in his ear.

Paladin turned back to his ear transceiver. "Max, come in! Max! What's your status?" No answer, then a high-pitched whine that made him pull the transceiver from his ear.

Polly, back in the hallway doorframe, called over to

149

Paladin. "Where's Bishop?"

"Our shooter's in the Philidor building across the street. I'm a sitting duck here." The Philidor building, once a popular hotel, was under construction for some new vision of the local land developers. That construction had lapsed and the building was now empty. There would be plenty of abandoned equipment to hide behind and openings for Bishop to fire from, and no people to interfere with him.

Polly went back to the short wave set and relayed the information. "Auntie on her way," he called to Paladin. "Seven minutes."

"Let's hope we can hold on that long," came Paladin's terse reply.

Another shot tore through the brick wall of the M & K Realty Office. This time, a hole of light opened up in the divan mere inches in front of Paladin's eyes, at the same level where he lay prone on the floor.

One more shot like that a few inches over, he thought, *will be the end of me.* He searched for a safe route to get out of the front room. At least the divan had provided some protection but that protection was gone now.

He rolled several feet to his left, then pulled his legs under him. With a lurch, he jumped forward toward the hallway. One shot. It only took one shot from Bishop. Paladin half-dove and was half thrown across the front room.

Polly reached out and grabbed one of Paladin's pant

leg, careful not to catch a bullet himself. Polly pulled
Paladin into the hallway and out of sight of the sniper.
"Paladin?" Polly called out. No answer. "Paladin?" he
called again.

Polly checked where Paladin was wounded. Paladin lay
face-up on the floor, a high-powered bullet hole in his
neck, blood splattered over a three-foot radius of the floor.

Polly gulped down some air and went into the back
office. He re-opened the short wave and forwarded the
message to home base: "Agent down, probably two."

A Trap is Sprung (Qxf3 …dxe5)

Seven minutes later, Auntie arrived across the street
from M & K Realty. She did not approach it directly. If the
sniper was still active, she would merely be one more
target. Polly had warned her that the shots were coming
from across the street, from the Philidor building.

Auntie approached the building by keeping close in its
shadow so that someone above could not see her. She
walked silently up the concrete stairs toward the second
floor. She was glad that she was wearing her mid-high
shoes: a habit rewarded. *Was Bishop waiting for her in ambush?*
Probably. A sniper shot? Not this close. Either way, she was
ready.

She reached the landing at the top of the stairs that
flattened out to a concrete floor: a window on the left side
and a doorway on the right.

A lone Mannlicher sniper rifle rested on the sill in the

151

window, which faced M&K Realty. The sniper rifle's telescopic sights glinted in the sunlight. *A fine weapon. No one around,* she thought. *He must have left that rifle out for me to find.*

She leaned slightly into the doorway so she could see into the room. All was barren on this side. *If he's in this room, he must be on the other side, out of sight. Or was he going to make me find him?*

She carefully entered the room to be able to see all of it. The room was devoid of furniture except for an ugly green couch behind a worn wooden coffee table. *There he was!*

A muscular black man in his mid-forties sitting on the couch. One scar above his eye caught her attention. After many years of searching and following his trail of death, she was at last face-to-face with the infamous Bishop. He sat relaxed, an old ugly-looking Luger in his hand aimed directly at her.

He scrutinized her up and down in a way she didn't like. He smiled. "*Gottverdammt, Fraulein!* Why didn't I have an Auntie like you?" He spoke with a slight German accent.

"Bishop." Her only reply.

"Did I interrupt your date?" He chuckled. "Surely *das ist* not your, ah...working attire." Although his banter was light, his eyes were hard and never left her for a split second. He could afford banter, afford to be at ease, because he held the gun.

152

"How *didst* you—a *fraulein*, a woman—ever get to be head of your own *Abteilung*, department? I assumed Auntie *wast* strictly a—how you say, a code name."

"I had to work twice as hard as any of the men. I had to prove myself twice to be as good as them. I think you'll find me to be more than enough for you."

Bishop smiled again, but then shrugged. "*So ist die Welt*. Such is the world." He gestured with his hand for her to give the purse to him. "Slowly," he said.

She moved toward him and put her purse on the coffee table. She stepped back with her hands clasped in front of her.

"You know, woman-who-bests-men," he started. He seemed to have dropped his accent. "I'm surprised that you fell for the Duke's trap so easily. I'm rather disappointed." He continued to stare at her while his other hand opened her purse, rummaged around a second, then withdrew a Springfield 1911 handgun. It fired 45 caliber rounds. He glanced over at the gun. "Oh, such a big gun!" He smiled. "Do you like them big?"

Auntie simply stared back.

"I would ask for your other gun, but…" He examined her figure in the red skin-tight dress, his eyes caressing her slowly. "Ach! But where would you put it?"

"We didn't fall for your trap--" she started to say.

"And yet here you are." Bishop put her purse on the coffee table and gripped the 1911. He lay his Luger gently on the coffee table alongside her purse. He noticed her eyes looking at the Luger. "What—this old thing? I've carried this Luger with me since the war." He tsked. "I guess such sentimentality will get me killed one day."

"No," she replied. "Sentimentality is not what's going to get you killed today."

"Oh yes?" he replied. "What's going to get me killed today? It doesn't look like it will be you, Fraulein."

"I *triggered* your trap so I could get to you." She paused. "You are too predictable—and arrogant. That was your downfall."

He smiled again. "Do tell me more." He aimed Auntie's 1911 directly at her.

"First, we heard about your plan through an old intel channel, one that both sides knew to be obsolete. That meant we were meant to find it. Second, you set up across the street from our safe house and took a few potshots at my operatives. I assume that was to get my attention. That was dumb, especially for you."

The Bishop showed his white teeth in a charming smile. "I am flattered. Throw a few shots your way and *voila!* Here you are."

"Did you have to kill my agent?"

"To be honest, my initial orders were only to draw you here, away from your leader. Then, when your agent killed one of theirs, they upped the ante." Bishop shrugged. "Paladin, I'm afraid, was the ante."

Her jaw tightened. She had worked with Paladin for several years. He was a good agent. He shouldn't have died that way. She could feel the heat of anger rising in her, but she maintained a straight face and continued. "And most important of all, you have a penchant for killing people with their own guns—an MO, one might say."

Bishop quit smiling. He knew what a predictable MO meant. It was like a tell in a poker game. It gave the person who knew the tell a distinct advantage. A predictable MO meant that you could walk into a trap of your own making.

Auntie smiled and spread her hands apart, revealing a small easily concealable Walther PPK.

One microsecond of surprise, then Bishop pulled the trigger on the 1911. *Click!* He pulled again. *Click!* It was empty.

"The heavier the gun, the harder it is to tell when it's not loaded, even for an experienced agent." Auntie's lips twisted up grimly.

Bishop snatched for the Luger on the coffee table. Auntie fired three shots before he could reach it: two to the chest, one to the head.

She stood still for a moment. then took a deep breath and moved to the body. She didn't expect to find anything useful, but she would check anyway. Car keys: he probably parked a few blocks away to hide his approach and walked here. A wallet with no ID (of course) but a large wad of Austrian schillings, French francs, and Deutsche marks. She pushed all that into her purse. Nothing else. Wait! In the jacket slung over the back of the couch, she found a ticket to Bellini's *Norma* playing at the Palais Garnier opera house tonight at 8 pm—only a few hours from now.

She tried to think about Bishop's actions. *Bishop must have planned on meeting his contact at the opera house. He planned to kill me and then meet his client. He figured he wouldn't have time to return to his base before doing that, so he carried the ticket with him. That meant his base was not close, perhaps not even in the city.*

Auntie looked around the room. *Department W will clean this up,* she thought, *and will search Bishop's car. Perhaps they can find his base and collect whatever intel was there.* Auntie expected to close out many old cases with what turned up at Bishop's base.

She walked past the sniper rifle on the window sill. *A trophy of a gun!* She deliberated about taking it, but she wouldn't put it past Bishop to booby-trap it. She'd let W deal with it. She stepped down the stairs, realizing she didn't have time to get to the gala.

Auntie continued in her head with next steps now that Bishop was dead. *The Duke and Countess didn't know that Bishop was dead yet. If she could get to the Garnier opera house in time, perhaps she could stop them with finality. If she moved fast...*

Auntie hurried across the street to the M & K Realty office. Polly saw her coming and opened the door.

"He's over here, ma'am," Polly said, indicating Paladin's body in the hallway.

She stared at Paladin's body, now letting anger and determination show on her face. "Have you called W yet?"

"Yes, ma'am., Polly replied.

"Good. Open a channel to headquarters."

Polly slipped into the backroom and fiddled with the short wave set. The panel was still up and the metering lights were on from the call he had made only a minute before.

A female voice came on the speakers. "Dispatch."

Auntie glanced at Polly before she spoke. "Sofia, send Clark to Safe House Two as soon as he can get there. Not Safe House Four. I repeat: Safe House Two." Tell him to come heavy. She and Clark had worked Bulgaria together. He was perfect for this kind of action.

Auntie continued, "Bishop is dead and we have a chance to counter-attack before they notice. Tell Clark to set his sights on the Palais Garnier. I'll meet him there in ten minutes."

"Yes, ma'am," Sofia replied.

"Have him bring me a few weapons with ammo. Oh, and give him a change of clothes for me. Pick something flexible. This dress looks great but doesn't help me now."

"Will do. Weapons and field clothes. Ten minutes," Sofia replied.

Auntie turned her attention to Polly, a wry smile on her face. "Welcome back from vacation."

"It's been busy," he replied dryly.

"Stay here and handle things with W Department. If there are any problems, which I doubt, run them past Sofia. She'll know whether to call me or forward it to someone else. Shrike is still in danger."

Polly's eyes widened. "Yes, ma'am!"

Auntie made one other call to Sofia. "Get me Shrike's agent-in-charge, whoever that is today."

"Hold, please," Sofia said. The line went silent for a moment.

Auntie worked in an intelligence organization that fought against domestic and foreign threats. The Prime Minister was protected by a special personal security squad, informally known as the Henhouse. It was their job to make sure no foxes entered the Henhouse. When the Prime Minister was out of home, as he was now in Paris, both Ops and the Henhouse were on high alert

These two organizations only bumped up against each other in dire situations such as this, so she didn't have first-hand experience of their inner workings.

Sofia's voice returned. "Connecting now to Rebel, agent-in-charge."

Auntie was relieved when Rebel answered the radio. She knew him by reputation. He kept close to the Prime Minister at all times; like lint, the other agents said. For Rebel to be charge now gave her some comfort because he was known to be one of the best.

Auntie spoke into the short wave microphone. "Rebel, Shrike is still in danger. Bishop is down but the Countess is still a threat, more directly now than ever. I think the Duke is directly involved in this too, so it's big."

Rebel contained his anger but it reflected in his voice. "I'd like to see her try. Give me a chance to get my hands on her. That goes for the Duke too."

Rebel's reputation preceded him. His hot temper could get the better of him. Sometimes he over-reacted, but in his job, an over-reaction was better than an under-reaction. He was loyal and sincerely cared about the Prime Minister. He was a damn good agent, even if sometimes a bit of a cowboy.

"I don't blame you," Auntie replied, "but we can't use Shrike as bait. I'm orchestrating a counter-attack. It's probably our best chance to stop this. Be prepared to move him if I call. Even if I don't call, move him if anything suspicious happens." She thought that last part was unnecessary. Rebel knew his job and would do whatever it took to protect his asset.

"Got it. Good luck." Rebel disconnected.

Auntie could almost hear him in her mind giving orders and moving people about, building a defense and updating the Prime Minister. They would be ready to move at a second's notice.

Counter-attack (Bc4 …Nf6)

Clark returned from an op in Jamaica less than 48 hours ago. It didn't pan out as expected, but a month in the Caribbean was never wasted. Time moved slower there. Even though nothing turned up, he was still adjusting to agency time. At the deliberate pace of all government jobs, it seemed that it pushed him along and yet he still rushed to catch up.

He only worked directly with Auntie once and knew

159

her to be direct and no-nonsense. He knew she was one of the best. Her ops ran with a watchmaker's precision. It was hard enough to become a female agent, almost unheard of, in fact. Women simply did not become leaders of her department without extraordinary skills and professionalism. It was not a position one attained by "sleeping their way to the top". That was a sure way to get killed when real skills were required.

Clark arrived at headquarters and sought out Sofia. He had worked with her several times before, but only through business, never personally; although he wouldn't have minded that.

Sofia had already packed black bags for him. She opened them and showed him what was inside; as expected, weapons.

She also gave him a gym bag. Before he could say anything, Sofia said, "Field clothes for Auntie."

Clark nodded. *Sofia is always prepared,* he thought.

One nylon black bag was long and distinctly shaped. It could only hold a sniper rifle or a golf club—and he knew it wasn't a golf club.

"I've packed all your favorite things," Sofia said with barely a smile."

"My old Bessy?" he asked smiling.

"Of course." Her smiled widen. "Now move it, mister!"

Clark nodded, then closed the bags that Sofia had passed to him, and left for Safe House Two as instructed.

Now there is another rare bird, Clark thought, thinking of Auntie and Sofia. *Sofia is smooth and proficient. I can see why Auntie selected her. No chatter, no gossip, no extraneous conversation —all business.* He wondered if she had ever been an agent herself, or wanted to be.

Several minutes later, Clark climbed the stairs to the upper floor of what appeared to be a dilapidated apartment building: Safe House Two. An elderly but savvy building supervisor managed the bottom floor of the building of short-term apartments, as cover.

Safe House Two was on the other side of the cove from Safe House Four, and much closer to the Palais Garnier opera house. The Palais Garnier was a historic opera house in Paris, built between 1861 and 1875. It was renowned for its opulent architecture and served as a major venue for ballet and opera performances.

When Clark arrived, no one was at the safe house; but then, he was two minutes early. He unpacked and assembled his sniper rifle. He had relied on "Bessy" many times in the past. It felt almost a part of him.

Clark examined the opera house. It was ornate: angel statues on the top of a curved dome, a series of large windows on the second floor, and a series of pillars along the ground level entrance that made an ornate facade in front of the lobby entrance.

He set his rifle's telescopic sights on the opera house about 800 yards away. He checked the flag on top for wind velocity; barely a breeze. *A long distance shot but easily doable,* he thought.

Through the scope, he saw the Duke's guard through the central window of the second floor of the Garnier. He slid the crosshairs onto the guard's head. *Ready for the shot.* He only needed Auntie to give the order.

Clark slid the scope's view slightly. He didn't see the Duke or the Countess. If something was going to happen there, he expected more support, more weaponry. *Oh, wait!* One of the Duke's captain-at-arms appeared, getting into position: a specialist bristling with weapons and emanating proficiency. *This man was not an ordinary member of the Duke's staff. Yes, something's going to happen.*

Preparing an Ambush (Qb3 …Qe7)

Auntie arrived on time, as she always did.

Clark was already in place. He stared through the scope of his high-powered rifle. He addressed Auntie without turning his head. "What you asked for is in the back room."

There Auntie found a case of ammo for various weapons. Two rifles leaned against the file cabinet: the standard Lee-Enfield SMLE rifle and a Belgian FN FAL, a candidate to be a standard-issue NATO weapon, if approved.

Although they were both good solid weapons, she twisted her lips when she saw them. *What was this, a field test?* She knew that the agency was deciding whether to keep the SMLE or replace it with the Belgian model as standard issue. It all depended on the Americans, but she didn't know why.

Why should her country abide by the decisions of a foreign nation even if they claimed to be allies? Was she supposed to use both rifles and report back? This is not a training op or a field test, she declared to herself. *This was a fight to stop a very determined and ruthless enemy.*

Then Auntie saw the EM-2 "bullpup", a semi-automatic assault rifle lying on the desk near the shortwave set. With the trigger in front of the breech, it was shorter than a standard rifle; but had the same barrel length, so it didn't sacrifice accuracy. It had lots of firepower for tight spaces and this one fired a barrage of bullets in seconds. She smiled. *Someone in Q Department must be looking out for me.*

A Colt 38 Special also lay on the desk near the house's short-wave set. This also was unusual. Then she realized that these weapons were Sofia's choices. They had discussed the Colt less than a week ago, with Auntie praising it highly to Sofia, despite it being American. Auntie decided not to ask her how she got her hands on these particular weapons. *Well done, Sofia.*

Auntie opened the gym bag containing her clothes and laid them out on a chair. She pulled off her dress and fancy underwear. She realized, with the blinds up, her nude form could be seen through the window, but she didn't care. *This safe house, being in an older building, didn't have the one-way glass that Safe House Four did. Better to have the visibility to see someone coming.*

She hung her bright red dress on a nearby bookshelf, aware that it could be seen from a distance through the window. Perhaps someone would waste a few shots on it thinking it was she, giving her precious time to return fire. That ploy had saved her a least once in the past.

Auntie put on her more appropriate underwear, form-fitting black pants, sweater, and rubber-soled running shoes. It was tight and she liked how it embraced her body. Auntie felt sleek and daring wearing it. She strapped her Colt holster around her waist. *Proper field garb!*

Auntie loaded the Enfield SMLE. *For distance*, she thought. She loaded the bullpup, *in case I need to engage the enemy up close in the opera house*. She loaded the Colt, *just because*, and placed it in the holster she now wore.

Auntie returned to the front room and Clark. She leaned the Enfield and bullpup against the nearby wall.

Still peering through the scope, Clark said, "The Duke is there—second floor middle—and they're fortifying the Garnier. His arms master is watching the front. They have more than enough firepower to protect the Duke. What else is going on?" He leaned back to give her access to the scope.

Auntie leaned down, and adjusted her eye to the scope. Peering through, she scanned for what she could see of the second floor of the opera house. Through the central window, she saw the Duke's personal guard—a typical beefy bodyguard type. She also saw a second man she didn't often see. He was huge, as large as a refrigerator.

"I see Blockhouse. Don't see the Duke right now. He probably walked out of sight so as not to be seen through the window."

She shifted the scope slightly. "Down in the lobby is Link, their master at arms."

"A double-cross?" Clark asked. "Avoid paying Bishop when he shows up for his money?"

Auntie carefully considered this for a moment. "You don't double-cross Bishop. You don't want someone like him coming back at you. Besides, Bishop wouldn't have lasted this long if that would work. He probably arranged the money transfer some other way. Something else is going on. We must assume it's related to the threat against Shrike."

"Why are they fortifying so soon? The performance is not for several hours. Bishop's not due yet," Clark asked. "Perhaps they found out that Bishop is dead already? A prearranged signal that didn't come?"

"Hmm. Don't think so...but they *may* be onto us already." Auntie glanced over at Clark. "As soon as we make a move, they'll know that Bishop didn't stop us." She looked back through the scope. "Aha! So...they've upped the stakes. The Countess has shown up."

A tall woman in a fashionable white pantsuit with a matching jacket came into view. Her face was long with sharp features and short black hair. From a distance, she could have been mistaken for a man. Auntie knew her as a ruthless enemy, merciless and commanding to her staff.

165

This was a woman Auntie could do without, and she would like to make that happen.

The Countess entered the lobby and spoke to Link. He nodded, then went out of view. A minute later Blockhouse joined the Countess and Link in the lobby. The Countess, Link beside her, and Blockhouse in front, stood in a row with guns ready.

Auntie could see them through the ornate glass entrance doors. *Someone trying to cross the lobby to get upstairs to the Duke would not find it easily done.* She relinquished the scope back to Clark. "Looks like we'll need a little more muscle too." She went into the back room. Clark heard her opening the shortwave set.

Fortifying (Nc3 ...c6)

Soon Clark and Auntie were joined by a slender man with a good smile. His hair was thick, black, and brushed back easily. He was handsome with a bit of caricature to his features. He brought coffee for three. "What do we have?"

Auntie took a cup and introduced them. "Agent Horis: Clark, our long-range man. Clark: Horis. Horis will help with any close-up work." Clark and Horis nodded to each other.

Clark stood up from his scope. He accepted the hot cup and took a sip, studying Horis for a long moment to remember him, so as not to shoot him later by mistake. Clark nodded again and returned to his scope.

166

"They're fortifying in the Palais Garnier. Not sure why," Clark offered.

Auntie looked through the scope again. "It looks like more of a defense than an offense. They may be building a fallback position now before an assault on Shrike later." Pause. She thought aloud. "Hmm, but they left the windows in view. They didn't even shut the curtains. I think maybe to draw us in: an ambush."

She continued, "I've called for Cobra to put a little pressure on them. If they're expecting us, let's give them something to catch their attention. Cobra should be in place in a few minutes. Auntie turned her attention to Horis.

Horis continued to smile. He saw the bullpup against the wall. "Is that for me?"

"If you wish," Auntie replied.

Horis picked up the gun. He examined it eagerly. "Wasn't sure I would ever get to use one of these in the field." He scanned the room through the sights in simulated aiming.

"More in the back," Auntie suggested.

Horis went into the back room where the Belgian FAL leaned against the filing cabinet. "We may already be in it," he called into the front room. "Someone's approaching."

Auntie moved into the back office so she could see better what Horis saw. Unlike the grand stone structures in the main boulevard, small clapboard buildings lined the alley behind the safe house. A man carrying an assault rifle

167

and with a pistol around his waist weaved in and out between the buildings, keeping close to those on his left. He was dressed informally, with two- or three-days growth of beard, hair long and unkempt. Auntie did not recognize him. *He looks like a drug dealer,* Auntie thought, *not an agent of a sovereign state. He's probably a free-lancer, or a local.*

Discovered (Bg5 …b5)

In the Opera house, Blockhouse called out to the Countess in a deep hoarse voice, as if he was unaccustomed to speaking, "They're here."

A moment later, bullets smashed through the ornate front door, shattering glass onto the lobby carpet. Cobra kept their attention as a distraction so Auntie could start her plan.

Blockhouse returned a few shots, but whoever was shooting was well concealed. The Countess joined Blockhouse, slightly behind and to the right, and both returned fire at the shooter outside.

More bullets whizzed over his head. Blockhouse realized they were going wide, to his right. He was not the target, the Countess was.

"Countess," he cried out. "They have you in their sights. You need to get out of sight. I'll keep them busy." *If that shooter would have been a sniper, they would have got you,"* Blockhouse thought.

The Countess stepped back, turned and whistled, sharp and loud, like a man hailing a New York City taxi.

One of her agents came through a door at the back of the lobby and stopped, waiting for instructions.

"Now," she said. The man nodded and disappeared behind the closing door.

"There seems to be only one," Blockhouse reported.

"This may not be the frontal assault that we were expecting but a diversion," the Countess replied. "They may attack from the rear. I've sent two agents to check out their probable rally point."

Blockhouse nodded. More shots thudded into the door and walls around them. Blockhouse was unalarmed. *Just another day at work*, he thought.

\- * \-

A second man popped into view in the back alley behind Safe House Two. He was in front of the first one that Horis had noticed. Two enemy agents now, armed and ready to assault the safe house. The second man was as scruffy as the first.

They look like private militia instead of trained agents, Horis thought. *Cheap and dispensable. Is that what the Duke is using these days? How many more might be out there?*

The two men shifted from one building to the next. The front man moved while the man behind covered him, then the rear man slipped forward while the other covered him. In such caterpillar-movement style, they closed on the house. They approached the courtyard below. They never

169

looked up. Auntie wondered if the two men knew they were being observed.

"I'll take care of this," Horis said. He checked the ammo in his bullpup once more, hugged it close and left the office. He silently descended the steps to ground level.

Auntie followed him as far as the front room. "Clark, can you get a shot on the two men in the courtyard?"

Clark swung his scope around. "No, not from here. They're concealed by the awning below."

"Okay. Horis is on his own then."

Courtyard Battle (Nxb5 ...cxb5)

Short bursts of gunfire erupted from below. The enemy agents hunkered behind cover and fired back toward the house. Auntie could not see Horis anywhere, but she knew the sound of the bullpup: short rapid bursts of staccato burping. The man closest stood up and fired several shots toward what looked like the windows on the floor below. Another short rapid burst from Horis. The grungy man in front twisted and fell back; his gun slid from his hand as he hit the concrete.

The second man fired again. One shot. Two. Then he stood up. Auntie did not hear further fire from the bullpup. Horis must be down.

The enemy gunman backed away from the building slightly, giving a clear view past the awning. He raised his head up to the front room and glared at Auntie, eyes narrowed and face tight. He aimed his pistol with both hands, directly at her.

New Position (Bxb5 ...Nbd7)

Before the two seconds required for him to aim expired, a sharp crack rang out. Clark had pivoted and shot downward. The man flew backward five feet and crashed into the concrete.

Auntie nodded to Clark. "Go check it out. I'll keep an eye on the Garnier."

Clark pulled his holstered pistol and ran down the stairs. Auntie could see him carefully approach the fallen agents and pull them out of sight. He called up to Auntie. "The new guy, Horis, is dead. These others are done too. Toss down my rifle. I have a perfect shot of the Duke from this angle, out a bit from the house."

Clark holstered his pistol and stood beneath the window. Auntie opened it and tossed the sniper rifle out and away from the awning. It dropped fifteen feet into Clark's hands. He went to a short retaining wall between two driveways. He flipped a metal garbage can upside-down and set the rifle on the three-foot wall and the garbage can. "I can see the Duke through the second floor window—clean shot. I can see the Countess partially through the Palais lobby door. Just say the word."

"Duke first!" Auntie said. "Let's end this now."

Clark put his eye back on the scope. His finger tightened on the trigger.

A beefy man with a thick beard—the bodyguard--

appeared in the second floor window and threw the curtains closed. The chance to kill the Duke closed with them.

Clark fired the shot anyway, hoping that the Duke stood where he was for that last second. Glass shattered and the curtains rippled. At the very least, perhaps he hit the bearded man instead.

"Shit!" Clark called up to Auntie. "One of the Duke's bodyguards got in the way. I don't have a shot now."

"Did he see you?"

"I don't think so, but I took the shot. Don't know if it hit. The Duke is behind closed doors again."

Boxed In (O-O-O …Rd8)

Auntie was on the short wave again. She talked with the agent in charge of the Prime Minister's special security detail. "Rebel, we need your help. The threat is concentrating at the Palais Garnier. Protect Shrike but make yourself available."

Auntie, an officer in Operations, didn't have the authority to order Rebel in PPS to do anything, but she was confident that he would respect her position at the front line. He knew that she had the most accurate and relevant information.

A strong male voice responded over the short wave set. "Moving Shrike to the Guest House. I'll be waiting." While the Prime Minister was in Paris, he had his own safe house—the Guest House. It came with good security; and close by, more security was available. If the situation got more extreme, then Shrike could be flown out of the country in a matter of minutes.

The Palais Garnier is less than a mile from the Guest House, Rebel thought. *Do they have a 20 on where the Guest House is? Perhaps that is why the enemy is concentrating in the Garnier. They are so close that if something happens, it will happen fast.*

Ten seconds later, a klaxon blared and the red emergency lights flashed in the Prime Minister's apartments. Rebel and a few of his men moved him into the safety of the Guest House behind three other personal guards. Rebel returned to stand guard outside. After a moment's thought, he dialed up a number.

"Grasshopper, this is Rebel leader. I may have to leave Shrike. You'll have to cover me. It'll be up to you."

A young female voice replied over the phone. "Yes, sir!" She knew better than to ask questions, but she seriously wondered if she was up to the task. For some time, she had been learning the protocols that was required for personal protection duty, but she had no real experience doing what Rebel did.

Rebel was slightly nervous about using an agent so new for what he had in mind. Although he had trained her and thought her to be ready, he recognized that new field work was unpredictable.

Rebel picked her because she had excelled in the field. He thought she would make an excellent replacement for him should the day come. *Today must be the day!* He smiled

173

wryly to himself.

Grasshopper had already donned her battle gear when she heard that action had started at Safe House Two. She instinctively checked her guns and ran the 500 feet to the Guest House.

_ * _

Cobra fired another shot into the Palais Garnier from his concealed position nearby. He could see Blockhouse at the lobby door. Part of the Countess was in view, but it was a tight shot. He couldn't quite take the time for a well-aimed shot with Blockhouse returning cover fire.

"You may have to back up Nick," the Countess said to Blockhouse. "He's protecting the Duke. They've found him and someone took a pot shot at him. Almost hit Nick. He's blocking their attack for now, but not for long."

"Countess," Blockhouse protested, "I can't leave here until you're safely away. Even ignoring the shooter out front, they still have that sniper that took the shot at the Duke. One lucky shot from him is all they need to..." He didn't finish the sentence. They both knew what that would mean.

Another voice called out from the earpiece in the Countess's ear. "Countess, let me help! I can't do anything from back here. Let's take them out together."

"You stay back there with the Duke, Billy, for now. Protect him. I'll see what I can do." Billy was in the hallway outside the Duke's second floor room as a defense

174

if somehow they breached the hallway and made for the Duke's room. Inside, Nick was last defense.

The Countess knew they were in tight straits. She assessed. *Blockhouse was blocked, and that shooter out front was putting pressure on the other side, pinning the Duke's bodyguard Nick. And somewhere a sniper was adding to the threat.*

The Countess called Nick's partner on a hand-held radio. "Rockslide, bees are swarming. Return to the hive. Bring your honey."

"Copy that," a steady voice replied. Within seconds, Rockslide, an athletic and fit man armed with a shotgun and a pistol on his hip, was beside Nick and the Duke.

Rockslide carried a Beretta 1301 semi-automatic shotgun that enabled him to empty its four-shot magazine in just one second. With a shorter barrel length than most shotguns, it was handy indoors, too.

If Auntie doesn't know that the Duke is backed up by both Nick and Rockslide above, and Blockhouse below, the Countess thought, *then we may have a chance to surprise her forces and turn the tables. Also, as a premium, the Duke is dangerous on his own, and adds to the firepower there.*

The Kitchen Sink (Rxd7 ...Rxd7)

Auntie heard the open radio conversation. She switched back to Rebel on the encrypted shortwave. "I think they've called reinforcements. The Duke is well guarded on the second floor and they're blocking us on all three approaches. Is Shrike safe?"

175

"Yes. No signs of a counter-attack here." Rebel took a deep breath. "But Auntie, if they're massing reinforcements, we have to stop them, stop them now."

"Rebel, your job is to protect Shrike." Auntie hung up.

Make sure the Prime Minister is safe, Rebel thought. *Well, he is safe. No threat here. When I leave, Grasshopper will play defense. They need help in the field.* Rebel called Grasshopper. "Now!" he shouted into the microphone, then he left his post.

Rebel sprinted for the Palais Garnier. He went the long way around to come up behind the building. He heard shots fire sporadically at the front of the opera house. He found the blind side of the old building and climbed to the roof, where he set up his ropes. Within seconds, he was harnessed and ready to drop. He looked around for the sniper on Auntie's team.

From behind his cover in the alley, Clark saw motion on the roof of the Palais. A man was fully in the open. He had ropes attached. Clark sighted him through his scope. He could pick off this person easily. The man stood up, looked directly at Clark, and gave him the thumbs up.

Okay, Clark thought. *What was he doing here? A friend?*

Rebel launched himself from the roof of the Palais Garner, out and down.

- * -

The Duke paced restlessly. He was tall and thin and moved with authority. His hair was streaked with grey and he sported a goatee of matching color. He spoke with an Austrian accent. "We are boxed up here like a bird in a cage," he complained. "Make some room. Where's the Countess?"

Before either of his guards could answer, the second floor window and closed curtains burst inward with a deafening crash. A man rolled on the floor and stood up, his guns blasting as he rose.

Rebel had swung out and down on his rope, which he made just long enough to reach the second floor from the roof, and propel him through the windows.

The bearded man Nick was hit twice before he could turn and fire, but it was too late. Rebel turned his attention to the Duke. *The Duke is mine!* Rebel thought.

Off to one side, Rockslide stepped forward and the room exploded with the sounds of a shotgun blast. The first shot picked Rebel off the ground, and the second blasted him back out the window through which he had come. He landed with a thud in the plaza below, and in front of the lobby.

In a fluid movement, Rockslide dropped the shotgun and pulled the Duke to the floor before the sniper outside could put a bullet through him. The curtains, and the Duke's cover, were gone.

Auntie knew that there was a low probability that a sniper shot would work now that the Duke was aware of it. She saw Rebel's failed attempt. She also saw it as an opportunity. "Clark! Go!"

177

Clark ran toward the Palais Garnier as fast as he could, his sniper rifle on the ground in the courtyard outside Safe House Two. Hopefully, Cobra would give him cover.

What Rockslide didn't know was that Auntie's sniper was not out there, but was sprinting toward the Palais Garnier as fast as he could.

Eye to Eye (Rd1 ...Qe6)

Grasshopper arrived at the Guest House breathing hard. When Rebel said 'Now', he meant *Now!* She ran through the protocols in her mind to make sure Shrike was unharmed. She spoke into the Guest House's video camera. "Round robin, round robin," she gave the passphrase.

To her surprise, she found herself looking at the face of the Prime Minister himself.

"We're fine. No excitement here," the Prime Minister assured her. "Thank you for responding so quickly, ah," he couldn't remember her name. She was young and pretty. Dark short hair with intense brown eyes. He would make sure to learn her name soon.

"Call me Grasshopper, sir."

"Okay. Ah, thanks, Grasshopper." Not exactly what he wanted to hear, but it would do for now. Since Rebel was gone, she returned to his pre-assigned position outside the Guest House. Nervously, her eyes darted around warily for trouble.

The Prime Minister was amazed at who was willing to

be trained to take a bullet for him. *Wasn't she too young for this kind of job?* He wasn't sure how comfortable he felt about this young woman protecting him from hardened assassins. *Was this a job for women? Yes, there was Auntie, he thought, but she was an exception. On the other hand,* he thought, *Rebel had trained this girl. He trusted Rebel so she must be qualified. He trusted Rebel, therefore he had to trust Grasshopper (funny name). I'll have to invite her for tea sometime soon, and get to know her better.*

- * -

Gunfire upstairs! In the Duke's rooms! The Countess rushed up the stairs with Blockhouse right behind her. Now that the Countess was out of sight, Blockhouse was no longer pinned by the shooter out front. He was freed up to help Nick, although he didn't know that Nick was already down.

In the second floor hallway, Billy was about to kick in the Duke's door to respond to all the gunshots. Blockhouse ran towards Billy. *Someone was needed to stop the shooter out front from freely entering the lobby.*

"Cover the lobby," Blockhouse shouted to Billy.

Billy glanced at the door to the Duke's room again, then saw that the Countess and Blockhouse would soon be entering that room. He dashed to the stairway down to the lobby.

The Countess and Blockhouse entered the Duke's room, wielding guns. The Duke sat on a chair out of sight

179

of the window, and Rockslide was reloading his shotgun. The action was over.

"I don't think the sniper is out there anymore," the Duke said calmly.

The Countess carefully looked out the window and scanned the buildings. In the distance, she saw Auntie in the second-story window of Safe House Two far down the block.

The Countess lifted her rifle. *This could stop right now if she could take down her nemesis.* She leaned against the window frame and aimed her shot, but she was not holding a sniper rifle. There was a good chance she would miss. She saw that Auntie was also aiming a rifle in her direction. No scope though, so also not a sniper rifle.

She fired anyway. The shots were wide. Auntie fired back: two bullets spattered into the brick of the opera house, but also wide. Only a lucky shot could win, but the Countess didn't feel like gambling today. She wanted to look Auntie in the eyes when she killed her.

Deadly Exchange (Bxd7 …Nxd7)

Clark climbed up the rusty fire escape ladder to the second floor of the opera building. He opened a grimy window and warily trotted down the narrow hallway. *Where were the guards? Perhaps they had been pulled out front by Cobra's diversion. Perhaps the Duke and Countess had not brought as much protection as he thought.*

As he moved, he mentally calculated where the Duke's

room position was based on his outside sighting: central outer room of the building.

Clark reached the door he figured was between him and the Duke, and probably a couple bodyguards. He took a deep breath and kicked in the door. It flew wide and he saw an athletic man with a shotgun peering the other way looking out the window, looking for snipers; perhaps watching Rebel on the ground below. The Duke sat on a nearby chair out of harm's way. The Countess and Blockhouse had returned to the lobby to check on Billy.

Clark fired the bullpup he had picked up from Horis in the courtyard. The sound of its short repeated bursts as it threw round after round filled the room. Rockslide tried to turn his shotgun on Clark, but he was contorted and twisted in a macabre imitation of a marionette gone wild as bullets tore through him. Rockslide fell to the floor against a wall under the window.

The Duke raised his weapon, but Clark swung the bullpup in his direction. Clark shook his head, smiling. "Don't do anything rash there, Dukey." He said with a sneer.

The Duke lowered his gun to the seat cushion of his chair. His eyes were hard and black.

"You've wasted a lot of good men, Dukey. It's time now for you to stop." Clark started to squeeze the trigger for the last few seconds of the Duke's life.

Clark had made the mistake of leaving his back to the door in a house full of enemy agents. His head exploded in light and darkness and searing red pain. He fell to the floor.

Hearing the shots in the lobby coming from the Duke's room, Blockhouse returned to the Duke's room as quickly and quietly as he could. Coming up behind the man aiming the rifle at the Duke, Blockhouse smashed him with a pistol butt from behind because he hadn't wanted to fire his weapon on the chance that he might hit the Duke.

Once the man was down, Blockhouse fired twice at the unconscious form on the floor.

Sacrifice (Qb8+ ...Nxb8)

Auntie could see the Countess in the Palais Garnier window on the second floor, but her rifle was not accurate enough. Clark had disappeared into the building and she didn't know what was happening there. She gave the Countess one last long-distance dagger-laden stare and left her position at the window. She opened a channel on the short wave.

"Rebel, Rebel, are you there?" Auntie called out.

To her surprise, a young female voice answered. "Negative. This is Grasshopper. Rebel has joined the fight. I have Shrike."

Damn! she swore under her breath. *Someone that young protecting the leader of our country?* "Is Shrike safe?" *She didn't know this person and who would give her a codename like 'Grasshopper'? What was that supposed to mean?*

182

On further thought, Auntie reflected, *Grasshopper was part of Rebel's detail and he would never put Shrike in harm's way with an under-trained or under-prepared agent. She'd must be good.*

"Shrike is safe. I am here and his guards are covering him," Grasshopper replied. "More are inside."

Auntie had no time for second guessing. "Look, Grasshopper, I am not your supervisor. Rebel is, so I can't command you to do anything, but I think Rebel was killed a few minutes ago. You have to decide this on your own, but it might be our only chance."

Grasshopper realized that she must be talking to Auntie. She knew about Auntie. Her reputation as a field agent was well known by everyone, friend and enemy alike. *No other female field agent would be giving orders. Rebel said to guard Shrike. She could not abandon her post, but...*she wavered. *I would not be abandoning my post. I have been* ordered *to leave my post and assist a field op. But wait...*she mentally paused again. *Auntie isn't my superior officer, so can she order me to leave my post?* Then she thought of Rebel, her leader and friend.

Auntie waited for a reply. A long silence came from the radio. "What do you need?" Grasshopper replied solemnly.

"Several of our agents have disappeared into the Palais Garnier. I think we have the enemy on the run. If Shrike is safe, I need you to enter the building and neutralize the Duke. The Countess too if you have a chance. I think their last agent is protecting him, but I will draw him out so you can get in. They won't expect you."

183

She paused, waiting for a reply. None came.

After a delay that Auntie found torturous, Grasshopper replied. "I understand, Auntie." Grasshopper did understand. She could continue doing her job, staying in position, or she could leave her position to join the fight. Shrike would be more vulnerable, maybe, but he seemed perfectly safe where he was. "Neutralize the Duke and Countess?" she asked. "You make it sound simple."

"It should be now," Auntie replied. "We've destroyed the Countess's forces and made a way for you. I'll pull their last guard out of position. We must stop this mayhem."

"Copy." Grasshopper was not as assured as her voice made it sound. She was a good field agent, but she always had backup before. She had never worked under or with Auntie, and personally didn't know how much to trust her intel. Grasshopper must rely on Auntie's reputation because stopping this attack was something that needed to be done.

Auntie threw the Lee-Enfield rifle strap over her shoulder and loaded her pockets with more ammo for both the rifle and her Colt. She ran down the back alley to a one-story building across from the Garnier, ran inside, and climbed to the roof. She knelt down behind a short brick wall that ran the perimeter of the roof.

Although the angle was strained, she sighted along the rifle and saw Blockhouse in the room with shards of window glass on the floor. Clark and another man lay on the floor, Rebel lay dead outside the lobby. The Duke was no where to be seen. *He must be out of range of the windows.*

It was a tight shot, only a partial view of Blockhouse, but she fired a single shot from her Enfield at him. He dove for cover. She methodically fired another shot. Leaning against the window frame, Blockhouse retaliated with a few quick shots. After a moment, no more shots.

Good, she thought. *He's coming after me.* She stayed on the roof and continued to fire into the Duke's quarters, not aiming especially hard. She intended to draw Blockhouse away so Grasshopper could do her job. *Grasshopper better be good!*

It didn't take long for Auntie to hear Blockhouse push through the roof door of her building. He scrambled behind one of the massive industrial air conditioning units.

Auntie left the rifle and pulled her Colt. She kept low and took cover behind a diesel generator. She saw a can of diesel fuel nearby. *She didn't want to be near that if it got hit by a stray bullet.*

She heard Blockhouse working toward her on one side of an air conditioning unit. She worked her way around to the other side to flank him. The gravel on the roof crunched beneath her feet, but she didn't know how much Blockhouse could hear.

She stopped, partly to avoid the noise of gravel beneath her feet, and partly to hear Blockhouse. She could not hear him. *Was he stopped and waiting for her? Was he being quiet and getting closer to her, to flank her?*

185

Auntie stepped back quietly and picked up the can of diesel fuel. She placed it slowly, cautiously, on the ground at the corner of the AC unit. He was sure to come around that side at any moment. She backed away and focused the Colt on the corner, waiting for him to appear, the fuel can in her sights.

"So I meet the infamous Auntie," a gruff voice spoke above her. Somehow, without any noise, he had climbed the AC unit and crawled over the top. An amazing feat for such a large man! He aimed his pistol down at her.

She jerked to the one side and rolled behind the generator. One bullet spat on the ground where she had been a half-second earlier; the other entered her shoulder. She stifled an outcry from the pain. Her breath came in gasps. She could almost fill her blood seeping into her lung as her breathing became more labored.

Stifling the pain, she ran around the generator. She heard Blockhouse jump down and run to the other side of it. She ran to the far side of the AC unit. He was still at the generator. She reached the corner where the can of diesel fuel was. She kicked a few pebbles of gravel, enough to make a sound that he could hear.

She pulled back away carefully from the AC unit, the fuel can in sight. There he was. She fired at the fuel can and it went up in orange fire and black smoke. Burning fuel splashed on Blockhouse and flames danced on his clothes. He tried to drop and roll. She stepped forward and fired a shot to finish the job, but he rolled away from her shot to a firing position.

She hit him once, but he fired twice. She gasped as two bullets caught her in the mid-section. She dropped to her knees as what felt like a train plowed into her. She was not able to breathe. Her last thought was hope that Grasshopper had enough time to get to the Duke and kill the bastard.

Blockhouse rolled again and put out the fire, but he was not able to rise. Her lucky bullet was solidly wedged in his chest. It would be a long death unless help came through that roof door. Whoever it was could be friend or foe: help or death. He pulled himself up to lean against the small wall along the roof perimeter, gun ready, and waited.

Grasshopper Leaps (Rd8#)

Grasshopper had decided. She hit the camera button outside the Guest House and told the guards that she would be leaving for a while to help Auntie's crew. After some initial surprise, they assured her that they could hold the Guest House without her until she returned. The Prime Minister encouraged her with "you do what you have to do."

She ran down the street, heart pumping with excitement and not a little fear, expecting a shot to tumble her to the ground any second. None came. She reached the backdoor of the Palais Garnier without incident. *Where were the bodyguards? Was Auntie right in that they were all gone, or was there still one left to finish her before she could get to the Duke?*

187

Grasshopper ran through the lobby and up the stairs to the second floor, as Auntie had briefed her. She reviewed her training in a flash of memory, took a deep breath, then entered the narrow hallway. One foot in front of another and crouching, she silently moved down toward the Duke's quarters.

The door was ajar. *The door was ajar?!* Grasshopper was shocked. She slowly peered around the doorframe and through the gap beside the door. She saw the walls pockmarked with bullet holes. Two men lay on the floor in a field of shattered glass, another dead against the wall. *What had happened here?*

She saw a handsome dark-haired man sitting calmly in a chair. *The Duke! The source of all our troubles!* she thought. He seemed relaxed, his hands in his lap, his gun on the coffee table easily within reach. *Perhaps he thinks everything is over.*

Her heart raced, her breathing labored. She took a deep breath and stepped inside with her back against the wall and the door to her right. Three men she didn't know —Nick, Rockslide, and Clark—lay prone on the floor within the room. *Where was Rebel?* She raised her gun and entered the room.

The Duke calmly looked at her, his eyes burning into hers. By reflex, Grasshopper focused on his eyes, then looked down again. With a slight shock, she realized his gun was now aimed upward at her, still in his lap.

"You don't want to do that!" She sounded stronger,

188

more determined, than she felt. The barrel of her gun was steady and aimed at the Duke's head. "Throw it."

The Duke shrugged. He tossed his gun to the side, where it slid beneath the nearby coffee table.

That was too easy. He was being unreasonably calm, Grasshopper thought. *What does he know that I don't? Perhaps he's expecting help to arrive. Are more agents on their way?*

The Countess stepped into the room, led by her own automatic weapon, but Grasshopper heard her. Grasshopper turned, stepped close and pushed the Countess's arm up, which knocked the Countess's shots high. Grasshopper grabbed the Countess's arm and wrestled with the Countess.

The Duke dropped to the floor to retrieve his gun beneath the table but Grasshopper struck out with a well-placed kick that knocked him back over the chair.

The Countess was shorter than Grasshopper, but stronger too. A bullet whizzed through the window and hit the Countess in the back. She screamed and fell to one knee. Cobra was still out there!

Grasshopper didn't know who shot that bullet. *Was it from a foe who missed her, or from a friend who intended to hit the Countess?*

The Countess twisted as she fell to the floor. She raised her gun to fire at Grasshopper on the way down. Grasshopper fired a quick shot into the Countess that hit her dead center. The Countess fell beside Clark, like two star-crossed lovers in a bed.

The Duke stood behind the chair, eyes wide. "Nooo!" He wailed. His mouth formed a little O, his eyes wide in shock when he saw his beloved Countess down. "No," he wailed.

Grasshopper gestured for the Duke to turn face down on the floor, her gun hand steady. She put her gun on the back of his neck as she pulled his hands behind his back and cuffed him.

"No," the Duke staid into the carpet on the floor.

Grasshopper called into her microphone. "Auntie, Grasshopper here."

No answer.

Grasshopper tried again. "Auntie? Anyone? This is Grasshopper. Come in please."

After some static and scraping sounds, a voice replied. "Auntie is not here. Identify yourself."

"I am with Shrike's personal security. I was working with Auntie. Who is this?"

"Auntie is not here. What is your message?"

Grasshopper didn't know what or how much to say. She didn't know who might be on the other end of the radio. "I have an important message for Auntie."

"This is M & K Realty. You must have the wrong number," the voice said.

Aha! Grasshopper knew M & K Realty was one of Operations' safe houses. She decided on a gamble. "There is no wrong number on a radio. Give me your codename, at least."

A long pause on the other end, then finally. "This is Polly of M & K Realty."

Grasshopper was relieved. *She knew that name. It was covered in the briefing when Shrike was brought over to visit in Paris. Polly and Max were the long-standing custodians of Safe House, ah,* she tried to remember, *Yes. Safe house Four.* She spoke into the microphone, "Message is: The Countess is down. The Duke is cuffed. Bring us in."

Plots from Literary Estates

Humorous Stories

The next story, *Mr. Berkley's New Slippers*, is actually a dream story. It came to me completely enough that I could have included it in the category with the other Dream Stories, but I think it fits this category better.

Mr. Berkley's New Slippers involves the ongoing problem of older people not being able to keep up with technology and how it pervades their normal lives. I still chuckle when I read it despite it being bad form to laugh at one's own jokes. Since my subconscious came up with it, perhaps it's okay.

The other story is a variant of the Shaggy Dog story, which are long-winded tales whose ending deserves a rimshot as it often ends with a pun. I use to collect Shaggy Dog stories for fun at parties and inflict them on the party-goers. I made this one up just because.

My Shaggy Dog story, *Ulysses and Cyclops*, is a variant on part of Homer's *The Odyssey*, where the hero Odysseus, also known as Ulysses, meets the giant Cyclops, also known as Polyphemus. As you may have suspected, there was more behind the story than Homer let on.

Plots from Literary Estates

Mr. Berkley's New Slippers

Mr. Berkley shuffled when he walked. Not just any shuffle, but a slow, painful-looking toe-to-heel kind of shuffle. He was old and his posture was bent. Mr. Berkley was long retired and had no job to go to, so he shuffled about the house all day.

Mrs. Berkley kept at activities in the house: baking, cleaning, and caring for Mr. Berkley. Sometimes a neighbor would see him, white-haired and slightly bent over, slowly shuffle down to the mailbox as if on a pilgrimage and say, "there goes poor ole Mr. Berkley," perhaps with a little pity in their voice.

With all the shuffling across the house floors, and occasionally down to the mailbox, eventually Mr. Berkley's slippers were worn through. He had worn large holes in them months earlier but continued to shuffle about in them.

His wife said, "We need to go shopping for you for new slippers. Those are ruined."

195

Mr. Berkley always had an excuse for this kind of outside activity, but mostly he didn't get new slippers because he didn't want to leave the house or shuffle about in public.

His daughters Miriam and Monica said, "Dad, you gotta get new slippers. Those are ruined." He only grunted. Then they told him about this new way of getting slippers without shuffling about in public.

"Order online," they said.

Finally, he didn't argue, so his daughters showed him how to buy a new pair of slippers. He ordered a pair of neon blue slippers in his size, appealingly labeled as *Autotronic Slippers for the New Age*, and thought that he was being "hip" and in vogue with all the young kids. He wanted to be included in the lives of his children.

A few weeks later, he shuffled down to the mailbox and retrieved a box with garish red, yellow, and blue wrapping. He shuffled back to the house.

"Where have you been?" his wife asked.

"I went out to play," he replied sarcastically. It was an old joke that at one time had been funny, but now had aged to a worn witticism. She knew he meant he went to the mailbox. He went nowhere else.

It being a sunny warm day, Mr. Berkley sat down on the front porch to try on the new slippers that had come in the multi-colored box. After he pulled away the wrapping, he saw that the slippers, a bright neon blue as ordered, were connected by a cord. He studied the cord for a moment.

He expected two slippers to be connected by a thin string, as is usual with buying a pair of footwear, but this cord was thick and bright white and plastic coated. It did not look like a normal string that held two slippers together. He thought about cutting the cord so he could put them on, but that would have required him to shuffle into the house, find the scissors, cut the cord, and then return the scissors. Too much work.

He procrastinated by reading the packaging that had surrounded the slippers. These modern slippers came with instructions! Mr. Berkley thought that was unusual, but then, he wasn't familiar with the new-fangled ways that the young seemed to know by instinct.

He skimmed the instructions. At the top, in bold letters that no one could miss (if they read the packaging) were the words "DO NOT CUT THE CORD". The instructions went on to explain that these were electronic slippers and the cord was necessary to keep them synchronized and offer complete worry-free control of the slippers.

As he was shifting the wrinkled packaging trying to read it, a black oval gizmo about the size of a small avocado dropped onto his lap. It was heavy plastic with a serious-looking red button in the center. The backside had two light-gray buttons. None of them had a description of what they were for.

He searched the instructions for what that ovoid could be and found a terse description. It was the remote control: the red button turned the slippers on and off.

197

Now that was a strange idea to Mr. Berkley: slippers that had to be turned on and off. He noted with slight amusement that batteries were not needed because these slippers, available only from Autotronic Slipper stores, came with a never-wear-out battery.

He put the instructions aside and put on the slippers. They were a perfect fit. He had worried about that at first. From what he could remember from years earlier when he had gone shopping at a store, it took many tries to get the right size.

He stood upright in the slippers, or at least as upright as his posture allowed. He shuffled about a few inches, one foot forward, then another. They felt good. He reached down and pushed the red button on the remote without picking it up. The slippers immediately vibrated and adjusted on his feet. They tipped backward slightly causing him to straighten up even more. These slippers had improved his posture!

He smiled to himself, deciding that some new-fangled things *are* worth having. He started to take a step forward on his right foot in his habitual shuffle, but the right slipper popped into the air to the length of its connecting cord; he was forced to bend his knee as the slipper rose. Then the slipper dropped and the left slipper popped into the air. Then it dropped and the right slipper snapped up again. These slippers high-stepped him down the walkway toward the mailbox.

He was out of reach of the remote after the first two steps. He tried to lean one way or the other but he only managed to turn onto the sidewalk near the tree lawn and proceed down the street. He felt a wave of panic when he realized that, according to the instructions, the batteries never wear out. *Where was he going?* he thought. *How long can he keep this up?*

"Someone help!" he shouted in his hoarse whispery voice, but no one was around to hear him. He continued down the street, first past Mrs. Gallagher's house, then past the Kearns family's house, and then many other neighbors. Soon he was out of sight of his own house and definitely out of reach of the remote that controlled these devil hooves.

If any neighbor was watching, they could see Mr. Berkley high-stepping in a parody of energetic marching band players at the city parade.

His daughter Miriam visited about this time. After greeting her mother, she asked where Dad was.

"Oh, he said he was going out to play," Mrs. Berkley replied.

Miriam stuck her head out the front door and saw the box on the front steps, now empty of slippers, and the black avocado-looking thing. She called out, "Dad?" but no answer. She put the black avocado-looking thing into the box, not realizing it was the powered remote for her dad's slippers. She closed the lid and put the box on a shelf in the front room.

"I don't see him," Miriam said, "I wonder where he could be."

"Well, don't worry," Mrs. Berkley said. "He couldn't

have gone far. You know how slow he walks anyway."

Little did she know that Mr. Berkley was almost a mile away and getter farther because he had, quite literally, stepped away.

Ulysses and Cyclops

You may have heard the story made famous by Homer's *The Odyssey* of how Ulysses met the giant Cyclops. He trapped Ulysses and his men in a cave and they escaped by blinding the cyclops and hiding beneath sheep. Well, that's not really what happened; I can tell you, 'cause I was there.

First of all, the cyclops's real name was Polyphemus, and he wasn't a giant, not the 20 or 30 or 40 foot creature that gets taller with each telling of the tale. He was a large brawny man, for sure, maybe seven feet, but he wasn't a giant-giant. And he hated the name Cyclops, which everyone liked to call him since he'd lost one eye in the war. He has a temper so don't ever call him Cyclops to his face.

Poly was glad to be away from the glares and taunts of people. He retired to a small island where he raised sheep, dates, and some of the greatest wine you'd ever want to taste. He lived well-enough in a cave in the mountain a couple hundred feet above the bay.

He kept a couple dozen sheep in a small pen inside the cave whenever the weather got cold or wet. The pen didn't do much since he left the gate open most of the time anyway, and the sheep wandered about the cave.

This is the part where Ulysses comes in. We called him Sly, because he was a devious captain. He was known to others as "The trickster of Troy," and he took it as a compliment.

Anyway, he and Poly met during one of the battles, but they were never enemies. In fact, after the war, we would play dice with him every so often, do some serious drinking, and spend some time away from the missus. It was about this time that Sly came up with his plan.

This is what he planned, and what we did. Once a month, we would ship out for a weekend fishing trip. We would fish all day Friday and Saturday morning, about the same amount of time it takes to get to Poly's island. We would play dice and get drunk on Poly's wine. We returned on Sunday, and if we were hung over, the wives just chalked it up to us being exhausted from fishing all weekend. Ha! After all, we did have some fish to show for it. We all thought it was a great plan.

Anyway, Saturday night we landed at his island and played dice. We drank his wine and ate his food in his cave, a warm place to play. He wasn't all that smart, so he usually lost a good bit of money too.

Then one evening, Poly got upset. He got on a rant about providing everything, and that we took all his money too.

"Let it go, Poly," Sly said. "Here, have a drink" and he pushed a flagon over to the big guy.

Poly got this idea stuck in his head and wouldn't let it go, as sometimes happens with not overly bright people. He insisted that we pay up for the wine and the food. Of course, we all laughed at this idea. We had been playing dice all summer and this was only a new objection for when he lost.

"Don't be a sore loser, Poly. You lost fair and square," Sly tried to reason with him, but in vain.

"No!" he insisted. "You come here every month and eat all my food, drink all my wine, and to add insult to injury, you take my money in this dice game. For all I know, it is rigged!" He threw the flagon of wine down. It splattered over the dice board and most of us. I got a face full because I was close to Sly.

"It is not rigged, Poly." Sly tried to sound calming, but he was also sloshed and it came off wrong to the angry giant. "You're just not a good player."

That was probably not the best thing to say at the time. Polyphemus stared and his jaw dropped. "Not a good--! Arghh! That does it!" He swept the dice off the board with one quick sweep of his massive hairy arm. "Pay up. You owe me half a year's work in food and wine, and you're not getting out of here until you pay up." He stood defiantly with his ham-fisted arms on his hips.

"C'mon, Poly. You're drunk," Sly replied. "We'll bring food next time, and some wine. Let's play." He motioned

to the men to pick up the dice and board that had
scattered across the floor.

I could see the wheels turning in Poly's head as he
thought about it. "No," he said finally. "You got all my
money." Then he started up again. "Your not leaving until
you pay up. All my money."

Now Sly started to get angry. He stood and faced the
big man. "Play was fair and square. If you don't want us
playing here, we won't come back, but you can't take back
your money just because you lost."

"No! You're not leaving until you pay up." He was so
out of it that he swayed on his feet.

"That's it. We're leaving." Sly turned to the crew.
"Pack up, guys. We're outta here."

Poly wobbled over to the doorway and stood in front
it. "Nope!"

So there we were. A giant of a man blocking our way,
and Sly and eight sailors bunched together behind him.
"Get outta the way, Poly."

"Uh-uh." Poly shook his head and burped. He was
looking a little green now.

Ulysses said back over his shoulder, "Let's go, men."
He pushed Poly as hard as he could sideways. It probably
wouldn't have done anything to a man Poly's size, but he
already had trouble standing. He stumbled and fell over
the fence for the sheep pen. We all ran from the cave.

We were a ragged bunch, being so drunk. We weaved
down the trail to our ship in the harbor. We ran as fast as
we could. On a good day, Poly could easily catch us, but

this wasn't a good day for any of us, with all the drinking and such. Gepson began to puke but he kept running. Poly burst from the cave bellowing.

He chased after us, kind of hobbling and burping at the same time. He would have caught us too, except that he stumbled again and fell into a big patch of poison ivy. He roared and came back on the trail, but began scratching on his arms and legs. Each time he scratched his legs, he paused and it slowed him down.

We made it back to the ship and sailed off. Poly finally bumbled down to the dock, but we were out of reach. Last I saw of him, he was jumping up and down in frustration, making the dock shake and sway. Now that we were safe, we all had a good laugh onboard.

We've not been back to play dice since then, and that was about a year ago. I don't know what would happen if we did. Has he simmered down yet, or is he still holding a grudge?

I don't know who made up that tall tale about a Cyclops and Ulysses fighting and hiding under sheep to escape. It made Cyclops sound like such a monster. My bet is Ulysses made it up to add to his fame. Ah well. To me it's simply one case where an itch in time saved nine.

Plots from Literary Estates

Science Fiction Stories

I am a great fan of science fiction. I loved it since I was a child. Robert Heinlein, Harlan Ellison, Arthur C. Clarke, Isaac Asimov and the other now-old-school authors who took me on fantasies of adventure using rational science for propulsion. Add a little humor and lots of action and you have the infamous space opera, or high fantasy in a sci-fi context.

Not to sound too out-dated, I also enjoy some of the modern speculative fiction writers, like Andy Weir (*The Martian*), cyberpunk novelist William Gibson (*Neuromancer*), Cixin Liu (*The Three-Body Problem*), and Daniel Suarez (*Daemon*). However, the following two stories follow more of the old style science fiction.

The first story in this category, *Ménage à Trois,* was also a dream story that I could have put into that category. The dream filled me with a feeling of loss and loneliness, a feeling so powerful I had to write it down. I hope that I passed that feeling on to my readers.

Ménage à Trois is a human drama set in a space station of the near future. What happens when a person is left alone too long? (Studies have shown that solitary confinement in prisons will literally drive a person crazy.)

What happens to the dreams and drives, the wants and desires of a person who is psychologically ill-fitted for that environment? I placed *Ménage à Trois* in the Science Fiction category, prioritizing its genre instead of its source.

The next story, *Fred,* is my oldest story. Its first draft goes back to my school writing class from years earlier. It could be called a space opera à la 1970's. I updated the original story using a style new to me borrowed from another writer, who received kudos and many awards for his first novel. I wanted to try that rather unorthodox style. I chose *Fred* as my target.

Ménage à Trois

Charlie felt alone. *You better get use to it*, he told himself. Charlie had almost a year left on his tour of duty on the space station where he worked. He performed the requisite experiments, measuring, calibrating, and pouring through vast amounts of data fourteen hours a day, which left eight hours a day for sleep in his personal pod, and an hour or two of private time during the day. He also spent his free time in his personal pod.

Charlie was accompanied by Mark and Alice. Mark was the medical officer: tall, handsome, and nice enough. Mark ensured that all the station inhabitants maintained their health and did not atrophy in the lack-of-gravity environment. He performed most of the people-oriented experiments at the station.

Alice was the astrophysicist. She was friendly and beautiful, with red hair and a bright face. She was the main reason Charlie spent most of his time in his personal pod.

209

She petrified him. When she aimed her bright white smile at him, his heart fluttered and his tongue tied.

Whenever either one of them was not face-in at their workstations, but moving past each other within the cabin, she would say "Hi." He would smile weakly and continue moving. She interpreted this behavior as that he preferred his alone time. She did not try to intrude.

Mark and Alice arrived a month after Charlie, so they had no way of knowing that he wanted to be part of the group, that he wanted to get closer to Mark and Alice, especially Alice. They had no way of knowing unless Charlie would tell them, but he couldn't get the words out. He was almost mute around Alice.

Often, Alice and Mark retreated together into Alice's pod for private time. He didn't try to eavesdrop, but he could hear Alice giggling—she had such a cute giggle—or Mark groaning. Sometimes she would moan. It drove him crazy thinking of her in there with Mark and not him.

Sometimes he turned on the atmospheric scrubber at the far end of the cabin for added noise, but there was only so many times he could run the scrubber without being suspicious.

Often Charlie would daydream about being on a date with Alice. He would be the center of her attention, as she of his. She would laugh at his jokes, discuss mutual likes and dislikes, and hold hands walking to her home. Outside her door, the goodnight kiss. He almost physically puckered his lips thinking about it.

System command management was almost paranoid

about any medical mishap occurring to one of the workers, therefore medical policy required that all station workers monitor each other's vital signs in rotation every three days. All station workers, including Charlie, were trained to do this. By taking turns recording each other's blood pressure, heart rate, respiration, temperature and other vitals, it was hard to hide a medical problem that a person may want to cover up. By rotating that assignment, it was unlikely that two workers would be in cahoots together.

During the appropriate times, Alice sat Charlie down and tried to make pleasantries with him as she took his vitals. She held his hand for pulse, squeezed his arm for blood pressure, or simply looked into his eyes. When his physical response included a quicker pulse or higher blood pressure, Alice took that as an acceptable state of Charlie's health, not that she was the cause of it.

When his responses to the conversation included only nods or shakes of the head or short awkward replies, Alice accepted that Charlie was simply a loner. She tried to understand that and treated him with friendliness. She apologized for being "in his space". Oh, how he wanted her to be much more in his space!

Alice lifted his arm to take his pulse. His heartbeat quickened as she held his wrist in her cool fingers. When she leaned in with her stethoscope, he could smell her light perfume. She was so close! He could feel a flush coming to his face.

"Well, Charlie," she said after a few minutes, "You have a little rise in blood pressure. Your pulse is elevated slightly too. I'll tell Mark to keep an eye on that." She smiled directly at him, raising two of his vitals all the more.

She didn't know that his pulse and his blood pressure also rose when he was taking Alice's vitals. She chatted on about how her experiments were going, the general quality of the station food, how beautiful the stars were outside without an atmosphere, and other cheerful tidbits.

She asked Charlie about his experiments. "Measuring the moon's atmosphere, right?" she asked archly.

Charlie only nodded. They both knew the moon had no atmosphere, but he didn't know what to say. He was just glad that she was lightly teasing him. She let him get on with his work. She knew he usually didn't say anything during the entire check-up.

One day Charlie overheard Mark and Alice talking. "I think Charlie has a crush on you," Mark said.

"What? On me? What makes you think so?" She replied in her sweet voice. "He doesn't say two sentences to me all week."

"You told me to watch his vitals," Mark said. "Last month, every time you gave him a check-up, his pulse and BP were elevated. That never happens during my check-ups." He paused and grinned, "Unless you're taking his vitals incorrectly."

"Pah!" She poked him playfully in the arm. "Taking vitals is easy. It's hard to take them incorrectly."

"Well, he does talk to me a bit," Mark continued. "Mostly about work. He is much quieter around you. Perhaps a schoolboy crush is what I'm thinking."

"What if I invited him to join our personal time?" she asked. "Do you think he'd do it? It would be pretty crowded in a single pod though."

"Sure. Why not?" Mark paused to consider. "Or perhaps he should join you alone?"

"He may be more comfortable with you there," she replied. "Since you say that he talks to you."

Mark shrugged.

Later that day, Alice stopped by Charlie's workstation. "Charlie?" she started.

He looked up and smiled slightly in reply.

"Mark and I wondered if you would like to join us tonight in my pod?" she continued.

"What?" Charlie couldn't imagine what she was asking.

"Well, you know that Mark and I get together in his pod. We thought you might like to join us."

"Aahh," he stammered. He would have to think about this. *Alice and Mark and him?* She was younger than he was, and he knew the younger culture was so much different, but Alice and Mark and him? "Aahh," he stared down at his workstation. "Meridian crossing tonight."

"Oh," she seemed disappointed. "Then perhaps tomorrow night?"

He partially shrugged and nodded his head. She took this as a likely yes. "Good! It'll be fun!" Her step was so jaunty that she almost bounced as she left his work area.

Charlie had lots to think about. *He would love to get together with Alice, but why Mark? Would they be doing what he*

213

thought they did almost every night? Could he bring himself to do it?
He would have to overcome a strong psychological barrier to join in
with them. He had fantasies of hand holding and kissing, but a
threesome? He was barely experienced with a twosome. Could he go
through with it?

Charlie spent the evening trying to focus on his work,
but his mind kept returning to Alice's pod, with Alice lying
inside. He wanted Alice to like him and he wanted to be
with her. Mark was a good guy but did Charlie want to
perform in a threesome? It was too bizarre.

The next evening, Alice stopped by his pod. She
knocked on the pod's frame. He slid the curtain aside.

"Coming?" she asked sweetly. She was wearing her
private-time attire: A white tank top with the standard
light grey shorts—very short shorts—of thin material with
no zippers, buttons, or clasps anywhere.

He nodded. She smiled, which sent a wave of heat
over him, then flounced down the cabin to her pod. She
glanced back to see if Charlie was coming and grinned
impishly.

He had not decided for sure what he was going to do,
or even if he wanted to proceed in this weird triangle
relationship. Just in case, he wore loose clothing that he
could easily remove.

He pulled back the curtain to Alice's pod and saw
Alice and Mark lying side by side with their clothes on,
watching the internet feed on the pod's computer. A video
was just starting. *Was the video important to what they were about*
to do, or was Mark passing time until they arrived?

Alice slid closer to Mark to make more room, but that resulted in little improvement. She patted part of the bed next to her, signaling Charlie to get in beside her. He folded himself in and couldn't help but lay pressed up against her, feeling her body warmth, unconsciously holding his breath. Slowly he relaxed, breathed easier, and lay happily in the confined quarters.

The video came up. It showed cats playing with other cats, cats falling off of furniture, or dogs and cats chasing objects and looking pathetic, or frowning or confused when something unexpected happened.

Alice giggled at many of these antics. Mark groaned when a cat fell with a bad splat. Alice moaned sympathetically at another mishap. Charlie realized these were the same sounds he had heard over the past few weeks.

"What?" he asked. "We're going to watch videos?"

"Certainly," Alice answered. "It's a good way to forget about work, and get to know each other better. There's always something funny on *Clickbait*." She turned and smiled at him, "Besides, it's kind of cozy in here now."

"Oh," Charlie said flatly.

"Didn't Alice tell you what we were going to watch?" Mark asked.

"No, she only invited me to come."

"What did you think we were going to do?" Mark asked.

Charlie realized he had extremely misunderstood what he had heard. "Well…." he was not sure what to say,

215

"Based on the sounds I heard from this pod from you two, I thought you were inviting me for a..a..."

"A what? You mean sex?" Alice tried to sit up in the tight confines. "A threesome? Ew! That's disgusting!" She jumped out of the pod and stood beside the curtain. She stared down at Charlie. "Ew!" she repeated with emphasis, and left. The curtain fell closed on Mark and Charlie.

Charlie closed his eyes in embarrassment. *Now Alice would never talk to him. She thought him a pervert!* A hole opened in his stomach and he felt like he was going to fall into it. *How had he botched this with her so thoroughly?*

He opened his eyes and blinked once. Then he blinked again and reality returned to him. He found himself alone in his own pod. Mark was not there. He opened the curtain to his pod and stared down the aisle to Alice's pod.

It was loaded with the boxes and devices that Charlie had put there last week, as a convenience before storing them in their proper places. Charlie felt alone—really, really alone. He sighed, and a tear formed on his cheek. He had daydreamed the whole event again. The video, her and Mark in the pod, her friendliness, sharing the pod together —the whole thing.

His memory reformed and the illusion was gone for now. Mark had had an acute appendicitis attack and both he and Alice returned to earth two months earlier. Charlie had been in the space station by himself since then, with only the clicking, hissing, and sighing of equipment in the cabin for company.

During the time they had shared the space station,

Charlie had never had a full conversation with Alice. He had tried, but could not muster the courage to talk to her. As her departure time came ever closer, he repeatedly resolved to approach her, to tell her how he felt; and every day he failed, until it was too late. Now she was gone and he had failed to say a proper goodbye.

He was closer to Alice in his fantasies than he was to her in real life. Every evening, he had almost the same fantasy: she invited him to share some time with her, and they were blissfully together, even if it was only to watch videos. In his illusions, which he could not control, she always slapped him when the threesome was mentioned.

Then he thought about this last illusion. *This time Alice had invited him into her pod and she hadn't slapped him as she had previously. Sure, she had stalked off, but things were progressing. Perhaps, with time, he could win Alice yet.*

Plots from Literary Estates

Fred

Scott and Fred zipped through space on their way home from an extended assignment in the asteroid belt when a highly unlikely event occurred: a meteor hit their spaceship.

Meteors move through space all the time with varying velocities and sizes. It would be unlikely for a ship *not* to encounter one, but this meteor was not a grain-of-sand-sized micro-meteor. That would not have been unlikely; that would have been common, so common as to be expected.

There are millions of micro-meteors flashing through space so their ship was built to prevent problems resulting from a micro-meteor collision. A micro-meteor would bounce off the ship's hull or at worst, if it were to puncture the hull, the anti-meteor self-sealing foam would have automatically prevented any problems for Scott and Fred. The ship's alarm system may not have even registered it.

This meteor was not an average-sized meteor, either. A meteor the size of a child's marble or as large as a softball could cause a problem. An average-sized meteor would be too large for the anti-meteor self-sealing foam to be effective. It could have punctured the hull and screamed through the ship. Of course, in outer space, no one can hear you scream, but Scott and Fred would hear it scream through the pressured atmosphere of their ship's cabin. That event would be unlikely, but not *highly* unlikely.

If the meteor was large, perhaps the size of a Volkswagen, and moving fast relative to Scott and Fred's spaceship, a high-speed collision would demolish the ship like a piñata at a child's birthday party. Scott, Fred, and the remains of their ship would have splattered into the recesses of space.

However, a meteor of that size would normally register on their ship's advanced-warning monitoring system. Scott and Fred could maneuver their ship out of harm's way, so a collision would be possible, but unlikely.

The event that actually occurred was a collision with a car-sized meteor that moved at almost the same speed and direction as their ship was moving. Of all the objects in space zipping along, any two that have similar speeds, direction, and size, and also colliding is *highly* unlikely. Even more unlikely is that the meteor approached at such as slow speed, relative to Fred and Scott's spaceship, that the alarm system mistakenly identified it as a docking craft, and remained silent.

A collision by this meteor imparted a catastrophic

momentum transfer to the ship. The meteor scraped along their ship's side like the Titanic iceberg, sheering a long gouge in the hull and rupturing the fuel tank. Instead of turning the ship into a piñata, it threw it off-course with a jolt like a billiard ball during the break. It's pressurized fuel system spouted fuel that acted like a retro rocket, continuing to drive it farther off course.

Scott and Fred were knocked about in the cabin and rendered unconscious. The ship flew off into barely-charted space. Although the self-sealing foam kept too much oxygen from leaking from the cabin, the nature of the fuel prevented the foam from sealing, and slowly the ship's fuel reserves dropped dangerously low.

Scott and Fred woke amidst the klaxons of alarms indicating the ship was off course, and the bells of imminent low fuel and oxygen. Being the professionals that they were, and familiar with crisis situations, Scott and Fred were not alarmed, only their ship.

Quickly they got the ship under control, switched the ruptured fuel tank lines to minimize fuel loss, and moved to patch the hull from oxygen loss. Scott searched the stars for either a place to land or a good trajectory to get them back on course. In this part of barely-charted space, there were not too many options.

"How bad are we?" Fred asked.

"Hmm. I don't think we have a favorable trajectory," Scott replied. "I found a small planet in range, and I think it contains enough hydride for us to make some temporary fuel. We'll have to take a chance and land there to know more. It's charted as an NL planet, NL-21345 specifically, but not much is recorded about it. Probably someone set up its profile in a flyby."

Fred trusted Scott immensely. If Scott said that was their best chance, then that was their best chance. "Okay," he said. "Let's put down."

Two hours later they settled on the ground of NL-21345. Scott looked through a porthole. The ground was rocky with sparse patches of green and yellow plants scattered across the surface. A tall mountain stood in the background. *This could be some place in Nevada*, Scott thought.

"Gravity close to earth normal, perhaps a little less. Temperature at 23.9 Celsius, so that's good. Oxygen levels are low though," Fred said, his face pushed against a device that read the outside atmospheric parameters. "I see nothing toxic, no strange pathogens. We could probably breath there for awhile but we'll have to use our suit oxy now and then to compensate."

"Okay," Scott nodded.. "How much time do you think we have?"

"Maybe eight to twelve hours of oxy left, not counting what we need to get back home. It depends on how fast we use it here. Maybe 15 minutes in the suit, 15 minutes native."

Scott nodded. "Hmm," he mused. "I'll get the fuel tank repaired and the converter set up if you can get us that hydride you talked about."

"No promises," Fred replied. "I'll see what I can find." He flicked a few levers, and read his scope again.

"There are strong indicators to the north. I'll check that way."

"Hold up a minute," Scott said. "Checking for a return path." He entered digits into one computer, then another one, flicked levers, and read another.

Scott's face was drawn. Fred knew that expression—it was bad news. "Yes?"

Scott went through his astrophysical ritual again. He stared for a moment while Fred anxiously waited.

"If we don't leave here in 15 hours, we won't have another viable path for over a month," Scott said eventually. "By that time, our oxy will be gone and our food will have run out."

Fred took a moment to absorb that. He gave a surly nod. "Okay, then we'd better get moving."

Both suited up for outside and stepped down the short ladder to the planet below. They looked like high-tech marshmallow men in their white space suits. They could not see each other behind their reflective helmets.

Fred opened his face plate to test the air. The suit was designed to turn off its oxy whenever the face plate was opened. Scott, from the safety inside his suit, watched.

Fred sniffed a little, then inhaled. "Smells a little funny, but seems okay."

"Fifteen minutes, then back on oxy." Scott said.

"Copy that. Let's get moving." Fred grabbed a few devices, including a bag and geology pick, and moved off toward the north.

Scott took a long toolbox and lay down under the ship

near the ruptured fuel tank. He pulled a torque hygrometer from the toolbox and read the tank. The reading matched what Fred had said. He lay the gauge down on the ground and went to work repairing the scars in the fuel tank with metal epoxy plates.

The repair was completed just as Fred returned. "Good news," Fred said, opening his helmet so he could be seen and heard better. "There's a shallow cave about 300 hundred yards that way. Inside, hydride is literally sitting on the surface. We can get all we want. In fact, we might want to claim this area as a hydride mine. Could be worth a fortune!"

To emphasize his point, he pulled a melon-sized rock of white puffy stuff from his bag. It looked like a head of cauliflower. "This should get us started!"

Scott stared at the rock that looked like a brain. "That's the largest chunk of hydride I've ever seen." He took it from Fred and held it up for a better look. Then he took the rock and laid it on the ground near the pressure gauge. "Tank's repaired. I'll set up the converter."

"I think it's time for Betsy to help out," Fred said, as he moved to a bin on the side of the ship. He pulled a small robot from the bin and placed it on the ground. It was about the size of a small doghouse, sported several antennae on top, and ran on treads. It had three robotic arms for dexterity work. He attached a couple of collection bags to its side. He grabbed the attached remote control device and strolled north. Betsy followed behind on her treads obediently, but slowly.

Within twenty minutes, Scott was feeding the hydride cauliflower into the converter, hearing the hum, and watching a light bluish liquid run through transparent lines from the converter into the fuel tank.

Fred appeared with two full collection bags. "I left Betsy working back there for now. Here's the hydride so far. I'm going back for more." He dumped the contents of his bag on the ground and went back toward the cave.

"I hope you're right about the air,' Scott said over his suit radio. "I feel a little woozy. I'm going inside." He quickly confirmed that the converter was running fine, and began to pack up his toolbox and stopped. There were two hygrometers on the ground.

That's strange, he thought. *Did I have a spare hygro? I don't remember that?* He threw both into the toolbox to investigate inside the ship.

Inside the ship, Scott examined both hygros. White powder flaked off into his hands as he handled one of them. *That wasn't suppose to happen!*

He tried to open the device by unscrewing the few screws that held it together. The screws were not real! It was like someone painted them onto the side plates of the gauge. Same with the needle of the gauge, although that was inside a glass tube. The gauge was almost as if someone had given him an identical non-working copy of the device when he wasn't looking.

Could something from the atmosphere have altered the composition of the gauge? He took a sample of the white powder that flaked everywhere from the device and examined it under his spectrometer.

What the blazes? This was not metal, but some fibrous material, almost white plant matter, except for some anomalous carbon-silicon ring molecules that he had never seen before.

Scott called on the radio to Fred. "Fred, I'm getting some crazy results here. Perhaps this place isn't as safe as we thought it was."

"What happened?"

"Nothing urgent," Scott replied. "I'll show you when you get back."

Fred returned a few minutes later and Scott explained the non-functional copy of his torque hygrometer and its strange composition.

"Weirdest thing I've ever seen," Fred said.

"And to add to the puzzle," Scott said, "Where did it come from? Did something on this planet reproduce my real gauge? If so, then this fake gauge was made in less than the 20 minutes that the real one sat on the ground." Scott shook his head. "Let's get that hydride and get off this rock!"

Fred operated the controller, programming Betsy to move into the cave, collect as much hydride as it could carry, and return. With a slight whirring sound and the light crunch of its treads on gravel, Betsy disappeared into the cave. Images from the video camera were redirected to the controller so both men could see what Betsy saw.

Scott, looking over Fred's shoulder, said "All right, no

surprises so far." Betsy continued down the tunnel path. Betsy's arms selected lumps of white hydride and put them into one of the bags on its side, then returned. "Nothing amiss here," Fred said.

Scott took the hydride and placed it into a bigger bag. They acquired many pounds of hydride rocks in a short time.

Fred took the programming console. Pushing buttons, he said, "I'm going to send it in deeper, places I was just beginning to examine." Betsy returned into the cave, her whirring echoing in the hollowness of the cave, then diminishing.

After Betsy's bag was full, it returned to the entrance of the cave. Scott emptied Betsy's latest haul into his bag. "I'm going to get this started in the converter," Scott said. He headed back to the ship.

As he fed hydride into the converter and gratefully watched the fuel stream into the ship's tank, he heard Fred over the radio.

"*Oh boy.*" It was not an excited "*oh boy!*" but an "oh, what have we now? "*oh boy.*"

"What's up?" Scott asked.

"Um, er..." Fred didn't say anything else.

"Fred?"

"Perhaps you should come here and see this."

That wasn't good, Scott thought. He almost ran to the cave entrance. Sitting there on the ground was Fred with Betsy's controller in his lap. At the mouth of the cave was Betsy, and another Betsy!

"Well," Fred said, as if he could say nothing else. "I guess we'll be able to collect twice as fast now."

Scott dumped hydride from the original Betsy into his big bag but when he tried to take hydride from the Betsy doppelganger, its collection bag and hydride were a single unit. There was a bas relief image of a full bag, like a sculpture, but no real hydride.

Scott rubbed his hands over the little robot. White fluff flaked off onto his gloves.

"But it moved! It returned to the entrance!" Fred objected. "How can it function?"

"Perhaps the replacement can do motion," Scott answered, "but is not smart enough to perform anything else. I expect that if I used the fake hygro on the tanks, it would not produce a reading. It obviously can't collect hydride."

"This little duplication act doesn't seem to be harmful," Fred said thoughtfully, "But just in case, let's make our fuel and get out of here. We need to report this. Let someone else investigate what in the world is going on here."

Several hours later, it was clear that although the converter was working flawlessly at its fastest rate, it would not be able to create a full tank in time. Scott calculated the return trajectory again from inside the ship.

"Yes, same as before." he told Fred over the radio. "We have about an hour left and then *we must leave*. The longer we stay, the more fuel it will take to get home. If we leave after that, we won't have enough fuel."

"Okay," Fred replied. "I'll send Betsy back with what we have so far because she's so slow. I will collect what I can by hand while she's crawling back."

Scott continued feeding the converter with hydride. When Betsy retuned half an hour later, he fed the hydride from her into the converter, then stowed Betsy in her compartment. Then he packed up the converter and prepared the ship for takeoff.

Scott sat in the captain's chair, double-checking the return trajectory and fuel predictions.

"Fred," Scott called out, "Let's go. We don't have any more time to convert your hydride to fuel now anyway. Get back to the ship asap! I'm starting the countdown."

"Coming," came the radio reply.

A few minutes later, the marshmallow man came bounding over the sparse ground toward the ship. He climbed into the ship and sat in the first seat near the door.

As soon as Scott saw him settle into the co-pilot seat, Scott closed the door hatch. He hit the ignition switch without waiting for Fred to buckle in. Fred knew what to do.

With a lurching roar and the sudden pressure of acceleration, the ship lifted off and blasted through the atmosphere into space. For long moments, both occupants were pushed into their seats. After what seemed like hours, but was actually mere minutes, the engines automatically kicked off, as they were programmed to do. The resulting silence was deafening.

Scott leaned forward to his instrument and breathed a

229

sigh of relief. "Whew! We made it. Right on course." He smiled and looked over at his co-pilot. "I was worried about that for a bit."

Then he noticed that Fred had not opened his face plate yet, nor had he buckled his safety straps for takeoff. Neither had Fred said anything, which was unusual for Fred. That is when Scott noticed the white flakey powder around Fred's seat.

What the blazes? Was this a doppelganger? He unstrapped and moved to what he hoped was still Fred. He tried to open the face plate, but the helmet was a single non-functioning piece. *Had he left Fred back on the planet?*

Out of reflex, thinking Fred might still on the planet, he looked through the porthole at NL-21345. He gasped at what he saw.

"No!" he cried out. "No! No! No!" He pounded on the porthole with his fist, until he finally slumped into his command chair, almost in shock. It was too late to turn back now.

Out the window, NL-21345 had turned into a planet-size head with a familiar face: big ears standing out, short reddish hair and freckles, and Fred's goofy gap-toothed grin. The entire planet had turned into Fred's face!

Gothic Stories

My daughter bought me a book of time travel stories written centuries ago in the gothic style: dark, foreboding, and often sinister or in macabre environments. Think H.P. Lovecraft, Verne, Poe, and H.G. Wells. Their style was so intriguing, I decided to try a few myself.

In *Staunton and His Two Brothers,* I took an old joke and rebuilt it as a dark vampire story as an experiment. I tried to follow the same Gothic style to produce the eerie vibe and mysterious characterizations that those stories use. Although the story is based on a joke, it is definitely not humorous.

In that same vein (pun not intended), with *Dark Explorers Adventurers Club,* I tried again from a different perspective. It is also Gothic but uses the old safari-journal style in which an innocent is involved with a much more driven and organized set of characters.

It seemed obvious that Staunton would become a member of the Dark Explorers Club. Let's hope that, like Staunton and his associates, it gets your blood pumping.

Staunton and His Two Brothers

The stranger stood in the doorway and scanned the patrons in the pub. He was dressed all in black. The regulars' lapse in conversation could have been explained by the interruption in their merriment, but it went on too long. Usually, conversations among the customers would not have wavered when someone entered, but this man in black brought a foreboding into the room with him. He was an intrusion on their evening, on their conversations with friends and fellow-drinkers. The silence in the room lingered.

The man scanned the room and made for the bar. He ordered three drinks, each in its own glass. The stranger fixed on the bartender as if daring him to challenge his choice. The puzzled bartender hesitated at first, then set three glasses on the bar. He poured amber liquid first into one glass, then the second, and then the third.

The stranger arranged the three glasses into a triangle

for easier carrying and carefully walked to a table near the corner. All eyes in the pub secretly followed every move the stranger made. The still-puzzled bartender watched the stranger take a sip from the first glass, then the second, and then the third.

The bartender watched the man perform this ritual twice more, then the bartender threw his bar towel over his shoulder and walked to the table. It was not something he wanted to do, but in all conscience, it was his duty as a bartender to offer his best service to his customers, regardless of how he felt about them.

"Excuse me, sir," the bartender said tentatively. "I don't mean to be telling you your business, but I think you would enjoy your drinks more if you ordered them one at a time. Each will stay cold and fresh instead of having all three sit out while you drink the other two. I will gladly bring them to the table for you if that would be of service."

The man uttered a deep and throaty chuckle. In a graavelly voice, as one who has spent many years without conversation, he said, "No, you don't understand. My name is Staunton. My two brothers and I have lived here in Ireland all our lives, until last month. My younger brother went off to America for an education, and my older brother went to Romania to become a vampire hunter. On the night they left, we agreed that each Saturday evening, I would have a drink with each of them, so to speak."

Staunton waved his hand at the three half-empty

glasses lined on the table. "And see, that is what I am doing."

The bartender nodded and smiled officiously, satisfied that the mysterious stranger was not quite so mysterious. The bartender returned to polishing glasses at the bar.

True to his word, Staunton showed up each Saturday evening for his three drinks. Although he attended regularly, he never fit in with the other regulars who frequented the establishment. He became a loner at the corner table each week and the other drinkers were happy to leave him to himself.

One evening four months later, the door to the pub flew open from a raging storm outside. Staunton stood in the doorway, silhouetted by the flashes of lightning behind him. He seemed to take no notice of the icy rain that smashed onto him. The room grew quickly colder, but not all of it could be accounted to the weather. Staunton slowly scanned the room and a grim smile crossed his face. He shut the door behind him, dripping puddles of water as he glided toward the bar.

There is something different about him tonight, the bartender thought. *He is Staunton, but not Staunton.* The bartender was further surprised when this new Staunton ordered only two drinks. The regulars, who normally would have ignored him after recognizing who had entered, also noticed something strange and dropped their conversation.

"One of his brothers must have died," they whispered to each other "but it's none of our business." They went back to tending to their conversations while keeping a subtle awareness on that corner table.

The bartender watched Staunton take his two glasses to his usual table, which now was reserved for him through sheer force of habit and the fact that no one else wanted to sit at the table after Staunton made it his domain. He began his now diminished ritual.

The bartender watched for a short time, trying to figure out what was different about his weekly customer. He could not put his finger on it, but it troubled him. Tonight, Staunton's table seemed to be the center of a cold circle of dark light. For no reason, the bartender felt a sense of dread in Staunton's direction. The other drinkers felt it too and began to leave the pub in twos and threes until the bartender was alone with the foreboding figure.

The same sense of duty that prompted the bartender to walk to Staunton's table on their first meeting drove the bartender to gather his courage to approach Staunton tonight. He wrestled with the decision for several minutes before he decided it would only be proper to offer his condolences to his customer. A quick "sorry for your loss" to do his duty and then he could retreat behind the safety of the bar and his whiskey bottles. He slung his bar towel over his shoulder and resolutely made his way to Staunton's table.

Staunton was staring at the two glasses of liquid as if deciding whether to drink them or not. Staunton had promised to drink to his brothers each week. The bartender couldn't guess what caused Staunton's hesitancy. Perhaps he was focused on his loss.

"Excuse me, Staunton," the bartender said with the proper apologetic frown when he reached the corner table. "I am dreadfully sorry for your loss."

Staunton slowly raised his eyes from the drinks lying on the table between his fingers and stared fixedly at the bartender, or perhaps more accurately, in the direction of the bartender. Staunton's face was pale and his eyes red-rimmed, as if he had been crying, which seemed appropriate to the bartender.

Staunton seemed confused. "Are you now?" he said as if he didn't quite believe the bartender. "What loss?"

The bartender thought he might have made a mistake. Close contact with this new Staunton unnerved him more than he would have guessed. The bartender gestured to the pair of drinks on the table. "Well, ah, you always order three drinks, but today you ordered two. I assumed that one of your brothers died, perhaps the one that went to Romania. Vampire hunting is an extremely dangerous profession."

At this, Staunton emitted a deep throaty chuckle. "Yes, it is, and my brother is most certainly dead now," Staunton replied. His chuckle twisted into a maniacal laugh, which opened his overly red lips to reveal two sharp gleaming fangs. He stood up to better reach his next meal. Amidst the howls and shrieks of the storm outside the pub, no one heard the screams from inside.

Plots from Literary Estates

Dark Explorers Adventurers Club

I was not going to write this story, but I am being forced to do so: an ironic task for the official archivist of the Club. I thought that if I wrote what happened on this last safari into the jungles of New Guinea, I would at best be not believed; and at worst, considered insane and end up in one of the asylums that such people who rant tales like this are placed into. That would be a better life than what is before me.

The story is bizarre and terrifying and unbelievable. It started out as only a job, but now my life depends on it. They are forcing me to do it, but that is not important to the story.

Desmond, Pierre, and Staunton co-own the Dark Explorers Adventuring Club, a posh old gentleman's kind of club on the upscale end of Manhattan. Earlier these three men organized a safari into the jungles of New Guinea—not an unusual adventure for members. I went

239

along to document the trip for Club records as I always do since I took the job.

Staunton hired a guide and several native load bearers. Our small group then marched into the humid, bug-infested jungle. First we followed a trail, then a footpath, and then veered off into sheer dense rainforest. Our guide hacked our way through the vines and underbrush with a machete for hours at a time.

The adventurers switched off and helped clear the trail. Instead of being fatigued by the grueling work, they seemed energized, which I thought was a typical reaction for those obsessed to achieve their goal.

I usually was not privy to where we were going, or how the safaris were funded, or the purpose of these excursions. The explorers were of the philosophy that the less I knew of our destination, the more objective I would be in recording the events.

I always assumed that the Club consisted of eccentric wealthy people who had nothing better to do with their time, those who spent an extravagant amount of time pursing their thrills. Now I know better.

We spent several days trekking through swamps and avoiding snakes. I cursed biting insects that persisted day and night. On the third day, we passed totems with human heads on them. This brought a smile to Staunton's face. It seemed he considered the totems as a measure of progress of some sort. To me, it seemed a warning from the indigenous tribes.

I had heard rumors at the port about vicious

headhunters living in these green wilds. More than one port official tried to discourage us from going along our planned route; Staunton encountered difficulty hiring locals as load bearers into the region. The Club had to pay double to get any bearers at all.

I should have stayed in the port or left New Guinea entirely, but I didn't know then what I know now; but that is not important to the story.

I will skip the events of the narrative that occurred while we traveled. The reader can find those details in any standard jungle adventure or safari document. It is sufficient to talk about the bizarre events after the headhunters captured us.

Less then one mile past the totems, our guide and the three bearers collapsed to the ground. Dead or merely unconscious, I couldn't tell. I never saw any of them again and never found out what happened to them. As I saw them fall, I felt a particularly sharp pain to my neck. At first I thought it to be an insect bite. Now I know that the pain was from a headhunter's poisoned blow dart, the main weapon used by the tribe of natives that we encountered.

It must have been hours later when blackness was replaced with a strong headache and the realization of the position we were in. Desmond, Pierre, Staunton, and I were tied to a stake in the middle of a small village of headhunters. About two dozen half-naked men and women laughed and cheered like they were celebrating a festival.

All the men and women's teeth were filed to sharp points, even several of the older children were so transformed. A massive stone pot mostly filled with water rested on a bonfire. Women and children threw in various vegetables as the water in the pot heated.

A brawny man with ugly scars across his naked torso stepped forward as I groaned on awakening. He wore a loincloth, a headdress of brightly colored feathers, and multicolored face paint. He smiled when he saw that I was awake. With a predatory grin, he ran his tongue across his pointy teeth, a gesture that made him appear shark-like and evil.

The three leaders of the Club were already conscious, if they had ever been unconscious at all. A brute of a man, who I assumed was the chief of the tribe, spoke to us in a kind of Pidgin English. I will not bother to try to reproduce that dialect here because it is not important to the story. I will just transfer the essence of the conversation.

"You have violated our sacred ways. You have come onto our land uninvited," he said in a harsh voice and with a sinister smile that I will never forget. He said this without inflection, a ritualistic reciting of the words. I had the feeling that no matter what we had done, he would find some excuse to kill us.

"We have caught you," he continued, "and it is customary that we eat you. Then we will skin you and use your skin to make our canoes." His lips parted as he laughed heartily.

242

"However, you are brave adventurers, so I will give you the honor of choosing how you die." He paused for effect and moved his eyes to a machete lying at the base of a nearby tree. "If you do not choose, I will hack you into pieces with your own machete. A gruesome and dishonorable death. Is that how you want to die?"

Desmond replied first in his precise English dialect. "Brave chief, you have caught us fair and square. As to how I want to die, I choose the pistol. The pistol is the only way for a proper English gentleman to die."

I was stunned on how these men faced death. No arguments, no defensiveness. I was also impressed.

The chief retrieved Desmond's pistol from his pack and loaded one bullet. He fired the bullet into Desmond's chest. Desmond gasped slightly and went limp on the post. He couldn't fall down because he was still tied to the post. His head flopped forward on his chest. The natives jumped up and down and cheered. More vegetables went into the pot.

The chief nodded an affirmation to himself when he saw the limp Desmond. He then stepped in front of Pierre. Pierre did not wilt under the chief's glare.

"*Sacré bleu!*" Pierre said. "Not a pistol! The only proper way for a Frenchman to die is by the sword!"

The chief retrieved Pierre's metal sliver of a sword from his pack and without ceremony, stabbed him through the chest.

Pierre uttered a loud cry into the wilderness, groaned painfully once, then twice, let escape a gargling gasp deep in his throat, and then went limp. As with Desmond, his head flopped forward on his chest while still tied to the post. Again, the natives jumped up and down, cheering. More vegetables went into the pot.

I was horrified. The half-naked chief walked farther down the post line to Staunton. After Staunton, I would be next. *How did I want to die? I didn't want to die.* These men impressed me at how casually they faced death but I didn't have the courage for that. I expected to be hacked mercilessly by the chief with the guide's machete. I could almost feel the blade sundering my limbs and neck. I knew I would cry or beg for mercy or even lose control of my bowels.

Staunton stared back at the chief. "And you," the chief said. "How do you want to die?"

"Of old age," Staunton snapped back with a wry grin.

The chief was undaunted. "You are as old you will get."

"In that case," Staunton replied calmly, "By the fork."

"What?" The chief was confused.

"Give me a fork. I want to die by fork," Staunton repeated.

The chief was baffled. He went through Staunton's pack but found no fork. Then the chief went through my mess kit and found one. He untied one of Staunton's hands and gave it to him.

To my surprise and the bewilderment of the entire tribe, Staunton poked the fork into himself in every place he could reach. Over and over he stabbed himself,

"Aha!" he shouted victoriously, "You may have me but I have your canoes!" Then he dropped the fork and his head fell forward onto his chest.

Surely he hadn't died from several dozen tine piercings. Had he passed out? Only on remembrance do I recall that no blood came from those wounds. The villagers cheered again when Staunton's head fell on his chest and more vegetables went into the pot.

After the cheering subsided, the chief approached me. I was sweating uncontrollably. "And you, small scrawny one, how do you want to die?"

My throat was dry and my tongue thick, but before I could reply, I heard what sounded like a soft chuckle come from Desmond's end of the post line. Then it was louder. Desmond lifted his head and chuckled visibly.

The startled chief stepped back. Then Pierre and Staunton lifted their heads and joined in. The chuckle grew into full out laughter, then the laughter grew sinister and darker until it was an outright evil cackle.

Staunton pulled his hands from the sinewy vines that bound him as effortlessly as if they were paper. He kicked his legs free, grabbed the chief, and bit him on the neck. The chief's blood gushed forward like a fountain. His struggling body twitched a few times then lay in Staunton's hands like a rag doll. Two tribesmen rushed to help their chief, but it was too late. Pierre and Desmond reached them first and blood spewed everywhere from the headhunters' bodies.

Staunton flung the chief's body through the air at the

cooking pot, knocking it over and causing a river of half-cooked vegetables and screaming terrified natives. Women grabbed their children and fled to the far end of the village. Some men picked up spears; others pulled the little blowguns they had used to capture us earlier. Although the natives got off a few shots, the Dark Adventurers showed no effect to the drug and no signs of slowing down. They laughed, red blood dripping from their fangs and soaking their clothes.

Many natives shook their spears and shouted *"Sanguma! Sanguma!"* The three vampires rushed with supernatural speed through the village, breaking necks and drinking blood from all who did not escape in time. I was happy to see that no children were caught in the massacre because the women fled into the jungle with them.

The village was now littered with blood-drenched corpses. The dark three, gore covering their shirtfronts, laughed and walked back toward me, as if they had just finished a rousing game of tennis.

"You really hammed it up, Pierre, in your death scene," Desmond said. "I had to stifle a laugh when you started that death gurgle."

"Ah! What can I say," Pierre replied. *"La vie n'est que théâtre."*

"And that fork bit!" Desmond said. "How did you come up with that? Brilliant!"

They grew serious as they approached me. They stared at me, still bound to the post. "Now, tell me, young Quincy," Staunton said, "What shall we do with you? What is your favorite way to die? You are an archivist, a documenter. Perhaps death by pen?" The others grinned at the jest.

"But I don't want to die," I said, stricken that I had known these men for almost a year, and now they turned out to be monsters, and monsters that would kill me without a second thought."

"Ah, but we all die. Well, some of us," Pierre replied. "It is a good thing, a gift, to chose how to die. Most people do not have such, let us say, luxury."

Staunton stuck his face close to mine. I could smell the blood. He reached a long-fingered nail, also covered with blood, toward my eye. "Now, young Quincy. You are an archivist, a recorder of adventures. You will write this story of all you saw and heard, all that we did. You will give it to me when you finish it."

He lowered his fingernail toward my cheek and drew a long scratch down one side. I felt the blood trickle down my neck. "And that is to help you remember!" he said as he wiped the blood from my cheek onto my forehead. "Right?"

"Yes, s-s-sir," I stammered.

He went behind me and I heard him snap the vines that held me, first my legs, then my arms. I was petrified, and could not help but fall on my face in the dirt. When I looked up and got to my feet, the three Dark Adventurers were gone.

I wondered when they would be back, but they did not return. After I composed myself, I left the village, relieved to be away from so much death and carnage. I made my way back to civilization, not sure of what to do next.

On the way back to the city, I realized I had no choice but to do what Staunton commanded: write this story. If I didn't, the scar on my face would remind me of my broken promise. *Was the scar some kind of marker for those vampires? A sign that the should kill me because I broke my promise? I could run, but they would find me. They had unlimited time to find me. Once they caught me, they would not make my death as quick as the chief's. It would certainly be much more painful. Would they turn me into one of them?*

What can I do against three creatures who go to the trouble of traveling hundreds of miles, trek through dangerous jungle, just to kill a village of people—as an entertainment, as a joke! They probably knew of the tribe's custom of allowing victims to choose their own death and had the whole affair planned out.

I had no choice. As I said earlier, my job as the Club's archivist is to record the adventures of its members. It is my duty to write the horrific incredible story you have just read, or I face something much worse. I know their secret. I am a prisoner of the Club. I must write their story and all the other ones yet to come.

I returned to the Club thirteen days exactly after the incident. The irony of thirteen days being an unlucky number did not escape me.

All three dark lords were drinking in the parlor and smoking cigars. I entered the parlor hesitantly.

Desmond greeted me with his customary silken voice, "Quincy, our archivist!" He sipped some kind of red drink from a glass. I didn't want to think about what it was. "How good of you to join us!"

I didn't know if I was being invited into their triad and neither did I know what would happen if I did not accept. I collapsed into one of the upholstered chairs in despair.

Staunton stared over at me for a moment, "Well, dear fellow, when can we expect to see your draft of our New Guinea adventure?" He took another sip of his drink.

"Why would you want me to write that story?" I asked timidly. "What good could come of it? Doesn't that expose you?"

"Why, to bring the others," Pierre admitted. "As word of these fantastic stories get out, others of our kind will join our Club. Our kind will come from around the world. We will be stronger with more members, would we not?" He smiled smugly.

"We do not bother about the exposure," Desmond said. "Those people who you seem to value so highly, they will find it too fantastic to be true. They do not *want* to believe. They do not want to leave the comfort of their world to face the *real* world. They will disbelieve whatever will interfere with that. We are safe enough."

Staunton turned slightly to address all of the others. "Well, there may be a few stalwarts that believe the story, but we can handle them if they come around."

"Aren't you forgetting about van Helsing? Drac had a *terrible* time with him." Pierre replied.

"Hmph!" Staunton scoffed.

I saw an opening, a small chance to get out of this situation. I sat on the edge of my chair. "Aren't you afraid someone will try to clear you out, shut down this Club? An organized killing party, perhaps?"

"Are you bothered by the death of a few primitive natives, Quincy?" Staunton interjected. "Is that what offends your tastes? Would you have us kill the local populace here in this fair city instead? The innocents in the street? The rich bankers, the powerful leaders, merchants, newsmen, and eventually policemen? That would be, ah…" he couldn't find the right word.

"Undignified?" Desmond offered.

"Yes, undignified," Staunton continued, "And definitely messy, with all the investigations that they would feel compelled to do."

"We try not to dine at home," Desmond added. "But we do want to find more of those like ourselves."

Silence enveloped the room. Cigar smoke rose slowly to the ceiling. "Well, Quincy, where is your first draft of our New Guinea adventure?"

I passed over the few sheaves of tear-stained paper that contained the tale you are now reading. What followed is not important to the story.

Historical Fiction

The following entry originated from an academic monograph some years ago, but because some of it was too controversial and some too hard to verify, it was never published. I converted it into this short story: *The Three Lives of Azul.*

The first part is an introduction by the translator of the content to come, written by Professor McCready in the style of translators of ancient works. He describes how three ancient Sumerian stelae—stone monoliths with writing on them— were found.

Writing on columns of clay or stone was a common way for kings in the 3rd millennium BCE to record their works for posterity; as King Gilgamesh did, who reigned in Mesopotamia about 2750 BCE. His stelae, or rather clay fragments of parts of them, were found in 1850 CE in the ruins of Nineveh. They confirmed his reign and his story, which is recorded in *The Epic of Gilgamesh.* (I used the translation by Stephen Mitchell, Free Press, 2004.)

The second part is what was on those monoliths, as written by Azul, the alias for an ancient Nephilim, or fallen angel. You can check that Nephilim existed in Genesis 6:1-4, or in my non-fiction book *Notes from an Analyst: Genesis 1 – 11.*

I have removed the academic references,

appendices, and special topics that accompanied the original work in order to provide a more seamless story.

The Three Lives of Azul

About the Translation and the Stelae

The Find: Mundigak, Afghanistan. August 1993

Thirty-four miles northwest of Kandahar, the crash of sandstone on sandstone from a nearby rockslide alerted two boys tending their goats. The plume of dust that arose in the morning light guided them to the spot. The rockslide was small, as measured by most rockslides in the mountainous terrain of this area, but the landscape fell away from an ancient opening that revealed a small cave in the slope of the mountain. Perhaps the slide started by happenstance, or perhaps because the sun warmed the rocks after the cold desert night, or perhaps angels moved the rocks. It's hard to say. The rockslide revealed a cavern room that had been sealed for centuries that may turn out to be one of the most important finds in archeology.

Leaving their goats behind, the boys investigated the

cave by the light of the rising sun that streamed through the entrance. They saw three tall pillars in the middle of a roughly circular room. They did not know that the pillars were ancient stelae.

Later measurements found that these three triangular-shaped pillars of rock, positioned in the center of a circular room roughly 60 feet (18.3 m) in diameter, are almost identical. Each are close in height, 11.7 feet (3.56 m) tall. Each pillar was formed into a triangular cross-section and smoothed on each side. On each flat face, 14 inches (0.356 m) wide, is inscribed proto-Sanskrit glyphs, which have been dated to the third millennium BCE.

The height of the stelae is exactly ten times the width of the writing surface, but the significance of this is unknown.

In addition, engineering experts found that the walls were inexplicably reinforced, presumably to help the room withstand earthquakes from below and the weight of the mountain above, but that is an educated guess.

The sandstone surface on the inside of the case was "glassed" by an intense heat at some time, the source and method of which remains unknown. Interestingly, the glassing is not as old as the pillars, which means that it happened sometime after the stelae were written and positioned.

The three stelae contain a continuous narrative that appears to be by a single author, known only by the pseudonym 'Azul'. Each stele represents a key "journal entry" of Azul's life. Only Stele I contains a brief reason as

254

to why the stelae are written, and why Azul used a pseudonym.

The glistening of the walls and the mystery of the writings seemed important to the boys, so they rushed to their village elders to announce their find.

Timing of the Find

The area where the cave was uncovered was strife with civil war at the time of the boys' discovery, and the locals and governments had more important matters at hand. Over a week elapsed before the elders investigated the boys' claims. It was four years after the elders reported the cave to their local officials that the Kandahar Provincial Museum sent Dr. Zarghona Ana, its archeological expert, to investigate. After another month, April 1997, Dr. Ana forwarded his findings to the National Museum in Kabul.

A team led by Dr. Marla Haussmann, working for the Kabul Museum, conducted a thorough investigation, including producing many high-resolution photographs. These photographs were sufficient to allow me to translate Azul's words. (The stelae have since been lost in the almost-total destruction of the Museum.)

Location of the Stelae

The importance of Azul's stelae consists not just in its contents but also in its location. Azul's room (as the cave with the stelae was soon called) was within a kilometer

from modern day Mundigak, one of the most popular
archeological sites in Afghanistan and arguably the world.
The Mundigak site contains a fairly well-preserved city
from the 3rd millennium BCE, as investigated by French
archeologist Jean Marie Casal in the 1950's. The location
of the stelae anywhere else makes it less likely that they
would be found.

Mundigak was large and prosperous in its day, as
indicated by having a temple and a palace. It may have
been one of the largest cities in the Indus Valley in its time.
Azul's room is on the outskirts of this city and Azul may
well have been a residence of Mundigak when the stelae
were written.

Contents of the Stelae

The first thing one notices is that although the stelae
are claimed to have been written by a single author, they
are in three slightly different languages: Sumerian (Stele I),
Harappan with a Sumerian dialect (Stele II), and Harappan
with an Assyrian dialect (Stele III).[1]

Secondly, the stelae describe events that span
centuries. If Azul was the single author, he or she was
extremely long-lived. The languages do support the
progression of Azul's life as described by the stelae.

The author of Stele I pre-dated the Indus Valley

---

1 The Sumerian and Assyrian dialects enabled Stelae II and III to
be translated because Harappan is still mostly undecipherable.

Civilization, c. 3300 – 1300 BCE. Azul claims to be one of the Fallen Angels after the war in Heaven, and later a Dasanu (semi-divine creatures most commonly referred to as Nephilim). He wandered to and fro on the earth for a time.

In Stele II, Azul was an ancient leader of a non-extant city of Harappa in the Mehrgarh Valley, part of the Indus Valley Civilization, probably c. 2600 BCE. The barbarian attack on the city of Harappa, mentioned in Stele II, occurred c. 2000 BCE. Later, Azul became a cohort of Nimrod about the time of the Tower of Babel (c. 5000 BCE).

Azul claims in Stele II to have written the *Rig Veda*, the most venerated and oldest of Hindu scriptures (c. 2nd millennium BCE), to enlighten his people with ideas about nature, theology, and cosmology. The *Rig Veda*'s historical origin is unknown to this day; perhaps Azul has answered this question.

Today, the *Rig Veda* is prohibited from being read except by the holiest of Hindu priests, because reading portions of it aloud with the proper syllables and the right tonal inflections might induce magic spells or miracles. See the Power of Word [Sanskrit VIBHUTI SABDAH] in the Special Topics section.[2]

Azul in Stelae III claims to have been a member of Nimrod's court, and part of the Assyrian conquests. He also references the Tower of Babel (c. 5000 BCE).

---

2 Ed. note: Special Topics section removed for this excerpt.

Plots from Literary Estates

Significance of Azul's Stelae

This translator examined the stelae's implications for
the modern reader, drawn from statements that Azul used.
Azul writes from the perspective of the ancient world of
the third millennium BCE, which offers a fascinating
glimpse into the persons and events referenced by the
scriptures of several major world religions.

The translator used Judaism, Christianity, and Islam as
comparisons. These implications, which may shed light on
issues that have puzzled scholars and theologians alike, are
captured in the Special Topics sections. A few such
implications include the supernatural Power of Word
(verbal blessing and cursing), the Flood, historical
locations such as Harappa of the ancient Indus Valley,
religious historical works like the *Rig Veda*, Nephilim like
Nimrod and Semiramis, the Tower of Babel, the longevity
of ancient patriarchs, and a look at the relations between
God, Satan, angels, and human beings. At most, Azul gives
us the perspective of an incarnation of a fallen angel; at
least, Azul gives us the perspective of a person of the
times.

If one assumes that the story written on the Azul
pillars is true, and weaves in matching historical references,
a rough sketch of Azul's life comes into view. Along with
the translation, the following work compares the narrative
with historical, archeological, and scriptural sources for
consistency among all of them.

One last point. Azul seems to be afraid of someone

called the Watchers. The stelae give no clue as to who or what the Watchers are. The only other known reference today is from the somewhat-discredited *Book of Enoch,* which refers to the Watcher as guards over the fallen angels on earth.

-- I. A. McCready
October 2020

Plots from Literary Estates

Text of the Azul Stelae

Translated from the Sanskrit
by Ian Alfred McCready

Stele I

These are the words of Azul written in my own hand. I
dare not reveal my true name. I run in fear for my life. I
fought valiantly during the war, reigned over cities, and
helped kings conquer nations, but eventually the Watchers
will find me. How can one such as I, who lived so bravely,
tremble now like a fawn in the eyes of a wolf? I write these
words in the time left to me to all who come after, not as a
defense or an excuse—God does not hear excuses—but to
express my regrets as a warning to others.

These are the words of Azul written in my own hand,
a captain who fought with valor and fierceness in the war
in Heaven, although I did not hold the cause in great
regard. What was the cause? Many of the Abhati [People
of the Light, immortal sons of God] disagreed with God's
plan to create mud people and allow them into Heaven.
Iblis in his pride decried that only the Abhati deserved a
place in Heaven. He gathered many tribes for his rebel
cause.

My tribe's leader pledged with Iblis, and so my tribe
joined the rebel faction. I did not care about mud people,
but what could I do but go along? A decision I now regret.

The rebels fought and lost. We are not made for
fighting nor was Heaven made as a battlefield. Only a
select

few were created as guardians of Heaven. Any of our group that confronted the guardian Michael was defeated without question. His weapons and powers outmatched ours in every way.

After the war, God created the mud people exactly as He said He would, according to His plan. He created them to resemble the Abhati, and He created them on the same prison planet to which the Fallen had been exiled.

These acts were intolerable insults to Iblis. Most who continued to be loyal to Iblis formed a new tribe and took an oath to desecrate the mud people. They vowed to force the mud people to lose favor with God, to be unfit to enter Heaven.

Although I fought in the war, as was my duty, I have no pact with Iblis. I chose to wander under my own counsel. I am not one of them. I am not involved. Someone tell the Watchers!

I was an Abhati on earth, wandering to and fro on that prison planet. I felt discomfort, as if I had lost something important, but could not recall exactly what that was. I recall little about those early days before earth. It is like a dream. I have the impression of great happiness and comfort, but about what, I know not.

I try to recall my lost life, to retain the images as from dreams, but what appears is not certain. Is the image in my mind part of the dream remembered or is it an image imagined? The impression is so strong that I want to dream again, but I am awake. It is no use.

In my wanderings, I would occasionally come upon a

mud person. They saw my light and were terrified. They fell into a swoon; or they fell to worship me, afraid for their lives. I do not want worship. I do not engage with them. Fortunately, I could appear to them or not, as I chose. Most of the time, I wandered the earth, veiled from the eyes of its inhabitants.

Sometimes I would come upon another Abhati. If he was a member of the tribe of Iblis, I would be treated badly, with great distrust and enmity. Many times I had to flee if more than one appeared together.

Sometimes I would come upon another Abhati, who was not part of the tribe of Iblis. Nevertheless, we still treated each other as stars passing in the night, passing at this point in time and space to move along, hoping never to see each other again. We are lone souls, which is part of our pain.

That was before the Watchers appeared, who traveled to and fro on the earth. The Watchers torment us whenever and wherever they find us, whether by assignment or by choice, I know not. They are powerful and cruel, usually traveling in twos. The war is over. Why can they not leave me in peace?

The Fallen discovered that they could infuse themselves into the mud people to create a Dasanu: Abhati light inside a clay vessel. Dasani are mortal but are much longer lived. They are superior to mud people in strength and size, but Dasani can communicate easier with—and are more accepted by—the mud people than those who show their naked Abhati light.

263

A fresh Dasanu may live a thousand years or more, but as they proceed through generations of clay, their life span deteriorates. The first mud person, created without a direct infusion, but only by the mere breath of God, lived for hundreds of years before his descendants deteriorated to the typical mud person's lifespan of three generations.

Mud people live within a glimpse of time and are without wisdom. They are easy to deceive and lead astray. Although mud people are in awe of Dasani, they are terrified of the native powers and Abhati form of the Fallen. The mud people believe that the Fallen are God, and Iblis's group is happy to let them believe that.

However, there are many Fallen, so the mud people believe that there are many gods. The mud people began to worship these false gods, which angered the true God mightily. God is a jealous and wrathful God.

The Fallen learned that they could desecrate their worshipers merely by being themselves, and directing the mud people into all sorts of depraved activity. The mud people enjoyed it and continued it. Iblis and his cohorts continued the deception to their benefit. By lack of wisdom, the mud people had ensnared themselves! It became harder for them to accept the truth. Iblis was succeeding in his vow: to desecrate God's chosen mud people to block them from Heaven, as God blocked the Fallen from Heaven.

God tried to reason with the mud people, to show them the error of their ways, but they are stubborn and arrogant. He decided to undo what He had created and eliminated them from the planet. He cleansed the earth with water, and eliminated all mud people and Dasani on it. How terrible it must have been for Him to destroy His great creation!

Although the Dasani died, the Abhati, being immortal, survived and made more Dasani after the Flood. It was also hard on me, who was not part of this grand conspiracy. I have never attempted to mislead or desecrate the mud people. Someone tell the Watchers!

Stele II

These are the words of Azul written in my own hand. I am now the former king and heir in the line of Princess Draupadi, who was created by the Power of Word by King Draupadi of Panchal. One of her five simultaneous Dasanu husbands (which one I must not reveal) was my great-grandfather. I am from a line of Abhati, and so my light is Abhati. I am also Dasanu.

I became a king of the mud people of the Mehrgarh Valley and reigned over them. I followed the wisdom of Krishna, whose counsel was passed down to me through the family. I guided my mud people to peace and harmony for many centuries. I am especially proud of my capital city of Harappa because it was prosperous, peace loving, and cultured.

Although there is much animosity between the mud people and the Fallen, I developed a small affection for them as their king. They are clever, persevering, and industrious, with a kind of loyalty.

I promoted peace, knowledge, and wisdom among them. I taught them about the cosmos and the world, about plants and animals, and how they might better survive on this prison planet.

I wrote in my own hand the *Rig Veda* for their enlightenment and understanding. At first, I dictated to my captains all that I willed because Abhati do not need to write. We are immortal and remember all things.

The mud people, who are short-lived and have memories like clouds in the sky, taught themselves to record their thoughts for later. They invented their own language to communicate past themselves to their children and children's children—a kind of immortality of their own. See, they are clever.

I, as Dasanu, have a long memory and a long life, but being in a clay vessel, I also suffer the ailments of clay, so some events in my memory pass. A clay body does not serve me as well as that to which I had grown accustomed. It is unreliable.

Once, the woman of one of my captains had a child, and I could not remember its name. When the captain reminded me, I was embarrassed. This was not the first time my memory had failed me, but I was determined that it would be the last.

I taught myself to write with some instruction from my captains. I am proud that I added the first and last books to the *Rig Veda* by my own hand. Although I learned to write to aid my memory, I use it now to spread

266

my thoughts when I am not present. I want to warn others, to spread wisdom, to announce to the world a caution to avoid the pain and mistakes of my life. God knows that I have helped his mud people and have not tried to desecrate them as Iblis tries to do. I have no pact with Iblis. Someone tell the Watchers!

I must write of the barbarians. I must explain my folly. My mud people lived in prosperity, and we lived peacefully among ourselves. They treated each other as they wanted to be treated themselves. We had no lawbreakers, no disobedience, except for that which stemmed from ignorance or immaturity.

One day, many tribes of barbarians flowed down from the mountains surrounding our valley and attacked my city and my mud people. They were a flood of ferocity and hatred. I did what I could to help during the attacks. I was a veteran of the War in Heaven in spirit, but that part of my life was gone. I did not teach war and fighting to my mud people. I did not want them to know the pain of contention and anguish that I had experienced.

My mud people knew nothing of war or fighting. They had no Astras [a divine or supernatural human missile weapon]. Indeed, they had no concept of weapons! They could, at best, defend themselves with hoe or pitchfork against the beasts, but they lacked the idea to retaliate against other mud people. They were slaughtered helplessly during their shock, and without mercy.

One part of me blames myself for not teaching them to defend themselves, but another part knows that a good civilization, in and of itself, does not need to know how to fight. That is what I thought before I learned the true nature of mud people.

The barbarians did not care about any of this. They destroyed the works of my people, defiled their women, and spoiled the fruits of my kingdom.

After my few Astras were gone, I fought with whatever implements I could find and bested many. Barbarian mud people fell to the left and the right, their blood flowed on the sand in rivulets, but they were too many. Eventually, my clay self was wounded and forced to hide in the hills. I listened despondently to the savage celebrations below. I wanted to avenge myself and my peaceful mud people who had suffered undeservedly. I sat stunned for several days in the cavern mouth that had become my impromptu shelter after the battle.

In the following weeks, I searched with grim determination for the Fallen Ones who had led these merciless attacks, or instigated them. After a time, I realized that there were no Fallen Ones behind the carnage. My blood ran cold at the thought of it. I couldn't believe it to be true: the barbarian mud people had initiated this atrocity on their own! Unthinkable! They lived for destruction and pain and evil. They needed no prompting from Iblis!

Mud people have an evil inside them that emerges when they are not shepherded. How long would I have lived in ignorance of their true nature? I decided that mud people were too wavering, too unreliable.

268

I realized that I had transformed only a small part of the Adamites [mud people descended from Adam] and taught them goodness and some small part of wisdom— but only temporarily.

My years of dedication to the mud people and my city were for naught. My good intentions were ripped away as the barbarians had ripped away my city. They would bring more evil into the world if left on their own. My sorrow turned to anger. Mud people should be removed from the earth! I set out in search of the one who could help me best eradicate them: Semiramis the Vanquisher.

Semiramis united her Dasani, and the mud people serving her, into the most powerful kingdom on earth. She waged war in Shinar from her kingdom of Babylonia. I traveled to the west and north, following tales from the trade caravans of her victories from nation to nation.

I arrived in Babylon, but Semiramis was gone long before; to where, no one knew. After she disappeared, her Dasanu son and consort Nimrod became king. He continued her campaign of terror, roaming the earth, conquering and destroying as many as he could in the same spirit of viciousness as Semiramis and Iblis.

Nimrod's ways of conquest were merciless and bloody. He used his powerful Astras and some Astras that Semiramis taught him. He seemed determined to eradicate or enslave whoever resisted him. They served him or they died, mud people and Dasani alike. No one could stand against him.

Nimrod destroyed the cities in Shinar and rebuilt them

to serve his purposes. The city of Babel and many more were razed and re-built with great citadels dedicated to him. His reign produced a populace of slaves that moved by his whim.

I decided that his goals fit well with mine, so I joined with him and supported his reign of terror. This was a mistake. I realize that now. Someone tell the Watchers!

Stele III

These are the words of Azul written in my own hand. I was formerly an advisor to Nimrod, king of the western world, and the fiercest of his generals; at least that was true at one time. I will not enter into Heaven from this incarnation. I damned myself during my time with Nimrod. I bow to God and ask for another chance to try again. I ask that I do not get locked in chains and darkness with some of the other Fallen Ones.

Nimrod demanded that the mud people obey him, but some stalwart souls protested and resisted. He smashed them down. He pulled his reins on them tighter, coercing them, either exiling all those who disagreed with him into the wilderness or killing them. He became a terror to the mud people and he knew no fear of God.

I shared in the destruction of God's mud people for years. I took pleasure in the blood of life that splattered in the dirt. I took pleasure in the slaughter that resulted when iron met flesh. I took pleasure in my revenge, clearing the earth of the foul fleshly creatures that had destroyed my city.

After a time, I realized that this revenge did not satisfy my soul. My beloved mud people were gone, as was that former life of gentleness and beauty that we had shared before. I grew to dislike the carnage that I led. I pulled back from Nimrod's campaigns of slaughter, and became more reluctant with each conquered city, with each tortured being. I regretted my part in Nimrod's conquests. I repented and no longer participated. I regret those actions of mine. Someone tell the Watchers!

I no longer shared Nimrod's fervor for destruction and so I lost favor with him. I did not support his obsessive killing and torturing with the same vigor as when we first met. My heat for revenge had cooled.

At first, I was an advisor ignored, the lowest state of affairs for an advisor. Anything I offered fell on deaf ears. Later, he excluded me from his inner circle and did not share his plans with me. He treated me like the least of his court.

Nimrod despised any being that claimed godhood or desired worship. Although he became the despot king of the western world, he never claimed godhood, and he hated those Abhati who did. He demanded that all beings make their fate by their own hands.

As a Dasanu, Nimrod knew he could not enter Heaven without God's approval. He endured one incarnation after another over the centuries without pleasing God. He declared to all that God had betrayed him and was not to be trusted. Nimrod could have been

271

the Light of Iblis himself!

Eventually, Nimrod had no one to attack. His conquests were finished, but he was not satisfied. Restless, He designed his Plan, a Plan that changed the world. He gathered the people of his nations to build a Tower higher than waters from any Flood, higher than any mountain, as high as Heaven itself. He decided to enter Heaven on his own, without God's permission or help. He would enter Heaven despite God!

My fever of revenge had subsided, and I came to myself. It occurred to me only then that mud people were not inherently evil, but inherently without wisdom. Mud people might be saved if they were taught wisdom and led in the right direction. I had already done that in Harappa. I might be able to do so again and salvage the mud people, and perhaps myself. Perhaps that would please God, and I could regain my place in Heaven.

I spoke out against Nimrod's Plan. I did not want to defy God. I wanted a chance to try again with the mud people as I had done centuries before. I went too far with Nimrod and he raged at me. I went from an insider in Nimrod's court to an outsider, and then to a person of suspicion. Being ignored is better: I had to take care for my life lest I inadvertently come upon him when he was in a killing mood. He grew worse when the Plan failed.

Dozens of nations and thousands of people worked together to build the Tower. Despite the people's fear of Nimrod, or because of it, they all worked together to erect the Tower. It was grinding and dangerous work, but everyone wanted the Tower because they thought it was a bridge they could use to traverse into Heaven. I doubt that Nimrod would have let them use it, but I know not.

During construction, God called Nimrod and told him to stop. He could not get into Heaven that way. Nimrod shouted back to God. Lightning flashed and thunder rumbled and the ground shook from the Power of their Words. The mud people of the plains were terrified and fled in panic; even the Dasani trembled and ran for cover.

God told Nimrod that he was ruining the earth. He was using his Power of Word for harm, turning forests into deserts, destroying entire lineages of people. He told Nimrod that He would remove the Power of Word from all creatures on the earth! Nimrod did not believe him, or did not care. He disregarded God and continued to build his Tower.

The next morning we all awoke. A kind of numbness had come to my brain. We spoke, but we could not understand each other. In anger, Nimrod tried to throw an Astra directly into Heaven, but his Word had no effect. He was furious! He tried again and again, one attempted Astra after another, but with no effect. Foolishness!

People babbled to each other, confused and dazed. Nimrod commanded them to add bricks to the Tower, but they did not understand him. In puzzlement, they wandered away, not sure what was happening.

I secretly tried my Astras, some boons and blessings, but with no result. I formed the sounds, but I was without power. Fear overcame me, the likes of which had never happened before. Perhaps the Judgment Day God had foretold had come upon us, I thought.

Nimrod, in his rage, saw me attempting VIBHUTIH SABDAH and blamed me for his Tower's failure. Perhaps he thought I had somehow caused the confusion that reigned. He ignored my protests and threatened to call the Watchers.

Whether or not he could summon the Watchers, I knew not. He did call the guards to have me burned. Fortunately, only a few of the guards understood him, and I escaped into the wilderness.

I decided to return to my Mehrgarh Valley, to my beloved Harappa, but when I arrived, barbarians still reigned. They had established and fortified my city as their own, centuries after their initial invasion. I knew I would not be able to live there, so I traveled south and took up residence in this city [Mundigak]. I decided to write down all that had happened to warn future generations.

I found a suitable cave, built appropriate pillars of knowledge, and began to write. I repent of my part in the war and my actions with Nimrod. I would have the mud people peaceable and prosperous again. I am on God's side, but I am tired, tired of this world and tired of running. Perhaps someone in the future will heed my message, and attempt to save the mud people from themselves. As for me, I will wait for the inevitable. I am ready. Someone tell the Watchers!

The Three Lives of Azul

Plots from Literary Estates

About the Author

Al Cline has had three professions in his life: software project manager, lecturer at several colleges, and now as writer.

Before corporate life, he tried writing. His first opus was a play for his local community theater.

After retiring from academic life, he returned to writing. His first book, *Agile Development in the Real World,* is about software project management.

His first novel. *Falsoon's Quest: From Shovel to Sword* is a young adult fantasy adventure using his experience writing fantasy role-playing game scripts.

His third book was an analysis of the first few chapters of Genesis (the most controversial chapters) in a collection of science-vs-Scripture gadfly questions.

You are now reading his fourth book. He lives with his family in Columbus, Ohio—a blessed bunch.

www.ingramcontent.com/pod-product-compliance
Lightning Source LLC
Chambersburg PA
CBHW050926030726

47503CB00007BB/2480